Araya's Addiction

Sempire Seductions, Book 1

Jocelyn Dex

Table of Contents

For Margie, my mommy.

Thank you for instilling in me a love for reading. And, thanks for not telling me I was too young to read your romance novels all those years ago even though I probably was. 😊 Lastly, finding your manuscript under the bed was what truly sparked the writing bug in me, so thank you for that too.

Blurb

She'd rather die than embrace her demon nature.
He'd rather save himself than help her.
Addiction is a bitch.

When Kean wakes up naked, collared, and locked in a cell, he knows thinking with his dick has gotten him into trouble. To gain his freedom, he must save a demon's life, but he has no intention of being some demon's errand boy.

Araya is dying. Sure, the naked guy on the floor can save her, but she doesn't want to be saved. Not by him. Not like that. No thanks. Upset by his eventual betrayal, she enacts a scheme to get him out of her life, but that scheme may awaken emotions that will bind them to each other forever.

Chapter One

Kean always knew his dick would get him in trouble. Tonight, it had. He'd been distracted by Talith, her blonde hair hanging past plump breasts to her tiny waist emphasizing her come-spread-me hips. Her body held promises of making his filthiest dreams come true. Sweet. He was in.

He should have known something was up. Should have known she wasn't human. Humans didn't look like that. Sirens, Sempires, Succubus yes. Humans no. *Please don't let her be a Sempire.* He didn't know what type of demon she was, but figured he'd find out soon enough.

He'd spent his entire life avoiding female demons. Yeah, he'd heard stories of the deliciousness of sex with demons, but he'd never wanted any part of that. Demons equaled trouble. He liked fun and sexual escapades with partners who weren't capable of ripping out his lungs after the fact.

Yeah, he'd fucked up royally tonight. Talith had walked up to him, smiled, introduced herself, crooked a finger and he'd followed her, expecting a night of unbelievable passion. The next thing he knew, he woke up here—naked and locked in a cell with some sort of metal collar around his neck.

For a cell, it was oddly comfortable, and the decor screamed porn set. Deep-red satin sheets draped the bed. A plush, navy-blue rug covered most of the floor. Fluffy handcuffs of blue and red hung on the back wall. A navy-blue leather recliner sat in the far-left corner next to a floor lamp that sported a red, fringed lamp shade. He discovered the small door in the right-hand corner led to a small but fully equipped bathroom, red and blue tiles adorning the floor and shower. He opened the mini fridge and saw it was stocked with small bottles of wine, water, and grapes.

Why someone would go to so much trouble to make a prisoner comfortable baffled him. Strange. The lingering smell of sex coating the air made him think this wouldn't be quite as bad as he'd first imagined.

Talith appeared before him. "I hope your accommodations are satisfactory."

"Not really my style," he said. "I don't generally wear a collar."

She smiled at his sarcasm. "Let's get right to it, shall we? My daughter requires your *assistance,* so to speak. Provide her with what she needs, and I'll set you free."

"What exactly does she need, and why the hell would I help you or her?"

She scowled, the air seeming to chill with her mood. "You will help her, because if you do not, you will die a slow, eventfully painful death." Instantly her smile and calmness returned. "You will also help her because it will be quite enjoyable for you. It's really a simple matter. Provide my daughter with your semen and you will be freed."

Um excuse you? Oh fuck. She must be a *Sempire.* Most demons exuded a unique vibe, but he'd never met a *Sempire* before now, so he hadn't recognized hers.

He wanted to confirm, but it seemed she thought him human, and he didn't want to give himself away by exposing his knowledge of demons. He didn't know if it would give him an advantage at some point.

He wasn't surprised she couldn't sense the demon in him. He'd met very few who'd been able to sense it. After all, he was only an eighth demon. His grandfather had been half-human, half-Incubus. He'd always considered himself lucky. If he had to be part demon, he figured Incubus, a sex demon, was a good one to be.

She motioned with her hand and instantly two hulk-looking clones—minus the green skin—appeared at her side. She continued when he only gaped at her. "Do we have an agreement?"

Kean loved a blow job as much as any guy, so loaning out his dick to gain his freedom should have sounded great, but it didn't. That this fucking *Sempire* had abducted him and locked him in a cell then demanded this of him pissed him off. He was no one's whore. Well, that was debatable, but he was a whore on his own terms, not some demon's. But, he didn't let on. He reined in his temper, grabbed his dick, gave her a cocky smile and said, "Semen, sure she can have all she wants."

Talith's smile faltered slightly, but she motioned to the guards again. One unlocked the cell, and the other entered and fastened a chain to his collar. Kean wanted to spring to action and crush the guard's skull, but he'd still have to make it past the other guard and Talith, and he had no idea if there were more guards beyond his sight. He was strong but he wasn't Superman.

He needed to be patient and look for his best shot at escape. Talith led the way up the stone stairs. One guard walked ahead of him, the other behind him holding onto the chain connected to his collar.

After exiting the porn prison, they passed several large, elaborately decorated rooms with a guard stationed outside each one. None of them seemed to find it odd to see a naked, chained man being led through the house. They came to a carved wooden staircase, made the trek up, and then took a left at the top. At the end of the long hallway, they stopped in front of a closed door with a four-inch-thick deadbolt on the outside.

Talith spoke. "My daughter is resting in here. You'll stay with her until she gets what she needs."

The bitch must be crazy. Chained or not, he'd have his get out of jail free card as soon as they left him alone with the daughter. As soon as he got his hands on her, he'd strangle her to unconsciousness and then offer Talith her daughter's life for his freedom. Clean. Simple.

One guard unlocked the door. The other shoved him into the room and surprise, this was his lucky day. The guard removed the chain from the collar. Apparently, he wouldn't be restrained. Were Sempires stupid?

"There is an intercom on the wall. Should you need anything, just buzz," Talith said.

"How about some clothes?" He didn't have a shy bone in his body, but once freed he didn't want to get arrested for streaking.

"Your services here don't require clothing," she said with a smile as she glanced at his cock. Then the guard closed and locked the door.

Kean looked around the enormous bedroom. The entire left wall was floor-to-ceiling windows, each framed with ornate gold molding. A king-size, canopied bed sat centered between the frames of the first window. Golden glass globe lights hung from the vaulted ceiling. Gold and green chairs of different shapes and sizes stood in various locations throughout the room. The largest flat-screen TV he'd ever seen hung on the wall to the right.

His gaze came back to the canopied bed. He'd missed her at first. He barely made out the small, sleeping form beneath the covers. His luck kept getting better. He stepped quietly to the bed and what he saw surprised him.

She lay on her side in the fetal position, her golden hair tangled behind her. She looked thin. Too thin and pale, and there were dark circles under her eyes. She looked so sickly he almost felt bad for what he was about to do. Almost.

He lunged and grabbed hold of her neck. That was the last thing he remembered as his entire body splintered from white hot pain as if shards of glass punctured his skin, veins, brain, muscles.

Kean's body ached in ways he'd never experienced—a burning, piercing agony. A groan escaped his lips as a cooling sensation comforted his neck, then his brow. He struggled to remember what he'd done to make himself feel so horrible. Had he pulled a massive drunk and this was the worst hangover of his life?

"Are you awake?" A small, feminine voice asked.

Wait. Had he brought a female home with him? No. He didn't bring females to his home. He went to theirs so he could get out when he wanted. He must be hung over at his latest conquest's home. Why couldn't he remember anything? He struggled to open his eyes. Damn things felt glued together.

He growled as soon as his eyes focused on the frail female bent over him and the memories flooded back to him. What the hell had happened? What had the demon done to him? And wait, why was she wiping him down with a damp cloth?

"What'd you do to me?" he croaked.

Her eyes widened. "Nothing," she said in a small voice, the weakness in it unmistakable.

"Bullshit." He tried to sit, up but his head pounded and spun so he stayed down.

"You'll feel better soon. Just don't try to hurt me again." She stood on shaky legs and ambled to the bed where she selected a pillow and brought it back to where he lay. She wore nothing but a short green satin robe. She helped him lift his head enough to slide the pillow under and then placed the damp cloth across his forehead.

The small effort she'd made seemed to have exhausted her. She sat on the floor a couple feet from him with her knees pulled to her chest, her chin resting on her knees and her breathing strained. He could snap her in half with two fingers.

"What's your name?" she asked him.

He ignored her question. "Shouldn't you be scared right now?"

Her lips lifted at the corners. "Scared of what? A helpless, naked man laid out on my floor?"

Oh yeah. He forgot he was naked. Hell, she could at least look a little embarrassed. But helpless? Him? Hell no. His male pride forced him to stand even though every muscle in his body screamed in protest, and his head felt as if an ice pick was being shoved into his gray matter. He swayed on his feet, but damn it he'd stay standing if it killed him. "Kean." He answered her earlier question through gritted teeth.

She clucked her tongue as she stood. To his satisfaction, she also swayed, although he didn't know why.

"I'm Araya. Why don't you have a seat before you fall?" she suggested. "I think I'll do the same." She moved to the bed and lay on her side facing him.

He chose the chair closest to him, not because it looked most comfortable, but because he felt he would collapse at any second.

Again he asked, "What did you do to me?"

She sighed. "It's the collar. As long as you don't try to harm me or my family, you won't experience that pain again." She frowned. "You're stronger than the others. They were out for at least an hour. You were only out for fifteen minutes."

Others? How many others had Talith brought here? And why? The girl was not a goddess like Talith, but she wasn't so unattractive that no man would submit to her without being abducted and collared. And her eyes... The golden color mesmerized him. He would fuck her if the circumstances of their meeting were different. He should have known mother *Sempire* wouldn't leave him alone with her daughter totally unprotected.

"What's wrong with you?" He didn't give a shit, but he needed to gather all the information he could.

She grimaced. "It doesn't matter."

"It matters to me. I'm the one who was abducted, shackled, and locked in this room with you."

"I'm sorry about that," she said. The sincerity in her voice surprised him. "My mother is determined to *help* me."

"And my semen will *help* you?"

Finally, she blushed. "I'm surprised she told you that much. She only told the others they were here to *service* me." She scrunched up her face in disgust. "What else did she tell you?"

"Nothing. Just told me to provide you with semen and she'll set me free."

"Then why did you try to hurt me?"

He shrugged. "I guess the same reason the others did."

"No. The others were more than willing to *service* me. When I refused them, they tried to..." She sighed. "Anyway, the collar laid them out, and after that they were so scared thankfully, they were removed from my room."

She eyed him with curiosity. "You don't seem surprised at my mother's request for you to provide me with... Well, you don't seem surprised." She looked away from him.

Oh shit. He forgot he wasn't supposed to know what she was. They thought he was only human. "Hey, for all I know, you're in some kind of kinky cult that requires members to, well, what are you supposed to do with my semen?"

She groaned as she pushed herself off the bed, muttering as she ambled past him and through a door at the far end of the room. "You wouldn't believe me if I told you."

He sat there trying to figure out what the hell was going on. Talith wanted him to provide her daughter with semen. He refused to be forced. His escape plan was foiled because of the damn collar. Probably forged by demon witches or some shit. And now, he couldn't even simply swallow his pride and whore himself out to gain his freedom because the female didn't want him anyway. Goddamn his luck.

Didn't want him. Why did that bother him?

Probably because he'd never met a female who didn't want him. His Incubus DNA made him virtually irresistible to women and unfortunately, *Sempires*.

He heard a crash come from behind the door she'd disappeared through at the end of the room. Oh well. Not his problem. When five minutes passed and she still hadn't come back, and he'd heard no more sounds, curiosity got the better of him.

He tried the doorknob. Locked. He knocked. No answer. He might only be an eighth demon but with that eighth came some benefits. Being inhumanly strong was one of them. He grasped the knob again and gave it a hard twist. It broke and he opened the door.

She lay on the floor, the green robe she wore hiked up showing the curve of her ass. Her perfectly round ass, he noted. She must have slipped as she was getting out of the shower and knocked over the soap dish. He crouched down and inspected her head the best he could without touching her. He damn sure didn't want to experience the pain of that collar again. He didn't see any blood.

"Hey. Wake up. You alive?" Kean asked.

Her eyes opened halfway. "Alive, yes," she said, her words barely audible.

SHE TURNED HER HEAD toward the sound of his voice. She was so tired. So weak. So cold.

She forced her eyelids up and her mouth dropped open at the sight before her. She took a deep breath and swallowed hard. He was squatting right next to her, his cock and balls hanging only inches from her face. In such close proximity, she could smell his semen. Tangy, spicy musk. Her mouth watered and her body screamed for her to take his cock into her mouth and draw out every drop, but her mind rebelled at the thought.

She hated her *Sempire* half. *Hated it*. Hated what it needed her to do. Had her father been a demon like her sister's father, things would be different. She wouldn't have the human half making her want things she couldn't have. A monogamous relationship. Love. She'd simply *feed* and complete the transition to full *Sempire*.

She'd thought she'd gotten lucky. *Sempires* didn't develop the need until their twenty-ninth birthdays. When she'd hit twenty-nine, she'd thought she was home free. Thought the *Sempire* need for semen had passed her by, that the human side had won, and she might be able to, one day, have the kind of life she wanted. But three months before her thirtieth birthday, it had started. The craving and hunger had struck with a vengeance then. But that didn't compare to the hunger she felt now.

She refused to succumb to her *Sempire* cravings, and she'd been weakening ever since. Her mother was desperate to get her to accept it, to get her to give in and take the *nourishment* she needed to survive. Hence, collaring men, stripping their clothing, and locking them in her room. For that matter, locking Araya in her room with nothing but tiny robes to cover herself.

The others were easy to resist. Attractive yes, but despicable. Showing the exact whorish traits that she tried to suppress in herself.

This one, she would resist him too, but he was different. Her mother outdid herself this time. Araya had never seen such a man. Tall, perfectly proportioned, and well-muscled. Black, silky hair that looked as if he simply raked his fingers through it to style it. The stubble on his face added to his ruggedness. And his eyes... The most startling eyes she'd ever seen. Pools of obsidian ringed with a sliver of silver.

Her body flamed, heat crawling from head to toe, as she realized she'd been unabashedly devouring him with her eyes. He must have noticed and enjoyed her appraisal because as her gaze dropped to his crotch again, his penis had become semi-erect.

"Do you like what you see?" he asked, a cocky grin on his face.

Oh god. The more excited he became, the more she detected the scent of his semen. The more she was able to scent him, the harder time she'd have refusing him if he decided to offer himself to her. She'd never scented the other men who'd been locked in her room. Of course, their balls hadn't hung inches from her face. That must be it.

She had to get up and get away from him. She'd never been so tempted to give in to her nature as she was in this moment. She turned away and tried to push herself up from the floor but she simply didn't have the strength and gave up.

"If I touch you, will this collar kick my ass again?" he asked.

"Only if you intend me harm."

She tensed when his hands grasped her under her arms.

"Relax. I'm only repaying the kindness."

When she looked at him blankly he explained. "The damp cloth. It helped."

Sparks of electricity danced on her skin where he touched her. He helped her stand, and when she was steady he let her go. She scolded herself for mourning the loss of his touch.

"I need to lie down," she said and unsteadily moved to the bed.

He sat in a chair next to the bed. "So what happened in there?"

"I slipped. Was too tired to get up."

"You didn't hurt yourself?" he asked.

"No. Just tired. Thanks for helping me up."

"Anytime," he replied.

She closed her eyes. So tired. The weakness got worse every day. She slept more and more, but only in short bouts, and wondered how much longer she would last.

Chapter Two

Kean noticed her beauty, for the first time, as he watched her sleep. The shower had added a little color to her cheeks and plumped her skin. Those effects had already diminished, but when he'd first seen her eyes, he'd been lost in their golden depths even when he'd still considered strangling her an option.

Those brilliant eyes had shocked him. Talith's eyes were gold, but not the stunning shade of Araya's. He'd never seen such a color. It was as though eighteen-carat gold irises contained twenty-four carat gold flecks.

She wasn't the perfect specimen like her mother. She was much too thin and pale, but through her damp robe he'd glimpsed her small breasts hosting perfect rosy nipples. The way she'd perused his body and how her mouth had dropped open as she'd studied his cock had excited him, and he'd wanted to spread her legs and fill her. Over and over.

Yeah, he came in here thinking no way in hell he'd be forced to *service* some *Sempire* but now, if she said the word, he knew he'd jump. What the hell was his problem? It must be that she didn't want him. He didn't mean to be cocky but getting females in bed or on the kitchen counter or outside a club wasn't a problem for him. Ever.

He jumped to his feet as a light knock sounded on the door. A second later, Talith walked in. She looked at him then looked at her daughter. Her expression turned dark. She crooked a finger at him, and he followed her out the door.

"I see you've not fulfilled your end of the agreement yet. I expected more from you."

"Hey, it's only been a couple hours. A guy needs time to finesse a lady," he said.

"My daughter is getting weaker with each hour that passes. Figure something out. She's running out of time," Talith demanded.

He wanted to ask why the girl didn't take the men Talith brought her. *Sempires* thrived on semen, so why the hell did this one refuse it? Of course he couldn't ask though or he'd give himself away. Instead he asked, "How is semen going to help her? That's a little weird."

Talith smiled a knowing smile. "Make it happen."

"You want me to force her?" he asked in disbelief.

Talith slapped him hard then quickly regained her composure. "I wouldn't allow you to hurt my daughter. I'm confident you're capable of getting the job done. Quickly."

If Talith knew what he was she would get him away from her daughter immediately. His father had warned him to avoid *Sempires* at all costs. Unfortunately for him, *Sempires* despised Incubi because of the danger they posed to them. Incubus semen was extremely addictive to *Sempires*. So, getting him away from her daughter might entail killing him, and that option didn't work for him.

The guard pushed him back into the room and locked the door.

He needed to get the fuck outta there, and fast. That meant he'd have to suck it up and help the surprisingly sweet little *Sempire*, but to help her he'd have to understand her resistance. With her sleeping so much and being so weak when awake it'd make it more difficult.

She slept quietly except for a few sighs and rolled over a couple times. The last movement caused the blanket to slip down and her robe to fall open, giving him a perfect view of one of her breasts. The small swell tipped with a delicious nipple called to him. He'd love to draw it into his mouth and tease it to attention.

Damn he was horny. His plans for getting laid last night had been ruined by Talith. Now, his cock twitched and demanded attention. It wasn't as if he had anything else to do while she slept. He gazed at her one last time, burning the tantalizing image into his mind and pulled the covers over her before strolling to the shower.

ARAYA STRETCHED HER arms over her head as she woke. She didn't feel as though she'd slept long. Her sleep patterns had been increasingly erratic the past month. She slept ten minutes here and thirty minutes there, but she was rarely awake more than thirty minutes at a time.

Her stomach rumbled, and her mouth watered. She hadn't eaten since yesterday and then only a couple pieces of fruit. She had less and less desire to force food into her body as the weakness overtook her. What was that delicious smell? Musky, tangy. *Oh god no.* She opened her eyes and jerked upright in bed looking around the room. She didn't see Kean but she knew that scent—his essence—tantalizing and beckoning her. Why could she scent him so well?

She slid off the bed, swaying as she did so, and the sound of water hit her ears as she noticed the bathroom door stood open. She'd close it and hope it diminished her ability to smell him. She'd go mad if it didn't.

She reached the door, and the sight that met her eyes almost floored her. Through the fog of the glass shower door, she watched his muscled form beneath the flow of water, his head bent forward, one hand pressed against the shower wall in front of him. The other hand gripped and stroked his shaft. He pumped it with long, slow strokes from base to tip, sometimes lingering at the head.

His eyes opened as if he sensed her presence, and he inclined his head toward her. She wanted to close the door, but the alluring scene held her captive, her feet frozen in place. He stopped stroking himself just long enough to slide open the shower door, giving her a completely unobstructed view of the water running down his muscled body, running off the thick head of his erection.

Not only did her mouth water, her pussy ached and flooded with desire.

He resumed the stroking, faster this time, sometimes breaking the motion to slide his fingers over his balls. She saw the muscles in his arm tense as he squeezed and stroked harder, faster.

His strained voice startled her out of her daze. "If you want it, hurry."

Araya took a step forward, wanting, needing, desiring. Instead, she jumped back and slammed the door shut between her and the temptation. She leaned against the door, breathing heavily. She'd never seen anything so intriguing, so beautiful, so freaking sexy. She'd almost lost herself. She'd never been so close to dropping to her knees and welcoming a hard, thick intrusion into her mouth and sucking until it filled her with liquid heaven.

She'd only touched herself a few times in her life, always afraid that anything sexual would make her prone to giving in to her *Sempire* nature, thereby completing her transformation and sealing her fate. She wanted to touch herself now. The heat and moisture between her legs were driving her crazy. She felt swollen and ached for release.

She fell backwards as the door opened, but Kean caught her and scooped her into his arms.

"What are you doing?" she asked.

"Carrying you to bed."

"Why?" she squeaked, cringing at the panic she heard in her voice.

"I'm a sucker for a female in need of an orgasm."

"What? I don't-I-" she sputtered.

"Either I'm giving you an orgasm or you're giving yourself one. But I won't be able to concentrate on anything else with the smell of your need clogging my brain. Your choice."

Wait? Humans could smell arousal? She thought that was a demon characteristic. Specifically sex demons. How humiliating.

He dumped her on the bed and said, "Which is it going to be?"

Oh no. He was serious. "I don't need *that*." She tried to deny her arousal. But then her gaze dropped to his cock, and the picture of him stroking himself flooded her memory, making her pussy clench. The scent of his semen called to her, ate at her resistance.

He inhaled deeply, and she'd swear his cock engorged more. Oh, how she wanted but couldn't allow herself to have. But maybe, maybe this one time she could allow the feel of a man's hands on her. As long as his semen didn't touch her body, surely she could control herself. She wanted to know how it felt to have a male bring her to orgasm before she died. He'd been unwilling at first but now he seemed quite willing to pleasure her.

"I can't," she breathed.

"*You* don't have to. I can take care of you."

He sat beside her on the bed. She knew she should run, crawl, scoot away. Something. But she was torn between fear and a desperate, consuming desire. She'd never experienced such a longing, such an urgency to have someone's hands on her until now. Could she allow his intimate touch? Just once, she told herself. Once did not make her a whore.

"You're in control. I won't do anything you don't want," he urged, his voice low and husky.

Just this once, she thought as she closed her eyes. Her life would be over soon anyway, and she wanted to know the feel of a male touching her, *this* male, caressing her, bringing her to that crescendo as her body burst into a million pieces. She spoke, her voice barely audible. "Hands only."

He didn't hesitate. The rough texture of his fingertips gliding lightly down her neck left flaming goose bumps in its wake. She tensed as he opened her robe to expose her breasts. A groan escaped her as he cupped them lightly and rubbed his thumbs across her nipples until they peaked into tight nubs.

His hands descended lower to her abdomen, to her belly, across her curls. She sucked in a breath and held it as his fingers found her clit swollen and ready.

"Damn you're wet," he said, his voice seductive, gravelly. He massaged the hard nub with slow swipes. It hadn't felt so incredible when she'd done it herself. The electric sensations speared throughout her body making her gasp for breath, making her muscles tense to the point of painful pleasure.

She jerked upright when he dipped a finger inside her. She'd never done that. She doubted it would have felt so wonderful had she done it herself. Kean's skills, though she had only her own to compare them to, rocked, made her senses reel.

She fell back as he began using his other hand to once again slide across her clit, as he slid another finger inside her. Oh god. She was going to die. Die from pleasure. Her hips ground against his fingers of their own accord, the tension building, tightening, increasing her pleasure.

"That's it. Come for me," he commanded her.

Her body obeyed. The first wave of release washed over her. Her body spasmed, and she cried out as she wondered if she would splinter apart from ecstasy. She rode his fingers as wave after wave of bliss crashed through her.

She calmed as the waves subsided and her body went limp. She couldn't bring herself to open her eyes. One, because that had burned every ounce of energy she'd had. Two, because she was embarrassed by what she'd allowed this man to do to her.

She felt the covers being pulled over her as she drifted to sleep.

Chapter Three

Holy fuck. That little *Sempire* embodied sexy when she came. Kean had used every molecule of restraint to keep from spreading her thighs and ramming his cock inside her, pounding and thrusting until they shattered in climax together. The way she gasped and moaned and ground herself on his fingers. Her small but perky breasts heaving with each ragged breath.

And damn. Her scent. What the fuck was that? His Incubus side made it easy for him to smell a woman's arousal but this female, this *Sempire*, gave off an intoxicating fragrance. He'd almost come immediately upon scenting her as he'd masturbated in the shower. It drew him in. Pulled at him. Clouded his mind with need. A need to please her before himself.

She'd come hard and her small form looked content and sated. *Yeah, I did that.* His ego was definitely boosted but now he needed to come. His balls ached and he'd have to resume using his hand. It pissed him off that she didn't want him. Correction, she damn well did want him, but she was set on denying it. He'd seen the hungry look on her face as she'd watched him in the shower. She'd wanted to take him into her mouth.

The thought of his cock in her mouth brought his attention back to the erection staring up at him. Maybe he would... No. He couldn't do that, could he? Talith told him to "make it happen". How could he make it happen without force—which he wouldn't do anyway? He wouldn't force a woman to do anything to him. He usually didn't even have to ask.

Frustrated in more ways than one, he stood and paced the room considering his options. *What options?* The situation sucked and not in the way he so enjoyed. She had wanted him. No doubt about it. Maybe he could wear down her resistance in time, but as Talith had mentioned, Araya was running out of time. If she died on his watch, he had no doubt Talith would kill him.

Fuck it. This was the best, more accurately *only*, idea he currently had. He sat on the bed careful not to disturb her.

He gripped his shaft and stroked hard invoking visions of her writhing at his touch. Visions of her slick pussy grinding on his fingers. Kean imagined how it would feel to replace his fingers with his cock in her tight depths. How it'd feel to have her pussy spasm and clench on him as she came while he pounded into her, his balls tightening until his own release exploded into her.

Oh fuck yeah. He stroked faster, his cock slick from droplets of pre-come that beaded at the thick head of his shaft. His release built in his balls. He barely held back a roar as he cupped the head of his dick, and semen jetted from the tip into his hand.

Kean fought the urge to collapse next to her on the bed. Not allowing himself to think about his next actions, he swiped his forefinger through the semen in his hand and reached it to her, hesitating only a second, before touching it to her lips.

He didn't move, afraid of what she'd do if she woke. Would she bite him? Slap him? Or beg him for more? He tensed as her tongue darted out of her mouth and licked her lips, a sigh escaping her.

He repeated the process, this time gently parting her lips and inserting his semen-coated finger into her mouth.

She still didn't wake, but her tongue slid across his finger and lapped at it hungrily. The feel of her tongue on his fingers made his cock jealous as again he gave her more. Her teeth clamped onto his finger and she sucked enthusiastically. He couldn't believe his cock was getting hard again, but the erotic site that played before him was such a fucking turn-on.

Her breathing deepened and she squirmed. He quickly pulled his hand from her and strode to the bathroom to clean himself. He marveled at how her lips had reddened and filled out in an instant. The color returning to her face as she'd sucked his finger.

Seeing the small, but instant, effect the miniscule amount of semen had on her, he really couldn't understand why the frail *Sempire* continued to reject what she so obviously needed. But he intended to find out. Soon.

He walked, hesitantly, back to her bedside. She hadn't awakened, but he'd swear a hint of a smile touched her lips. He settled into a chair, getting as comfortable as possible and closed his eyes.

ARAYA'S EYES POPPED open to the sight of Kean sitting in the chair next to her bed. Her face instantly burned as she remembered the intimate way she'd let him touch her. She'd been out of her mind with want. With need. For *him*. God, she'd never allowed herself to even kiss a man. What had she been thinking? She hadn't been thinking. That was the problem. *He* was the problem.

What about him threatened her resolve? Yeah, he was a stunning man, but living in a house with a *Sempire* mother and a *Sempire* sister, she'd seen hundreds of stunning men. Probably thousands.

She lowered her eyes and tried to will her facial temperature to return to normal.

"Good sleep?" he asked.

She didn't look at him as she answered quietly. "Yes. Did I sleep long?"

"About eight hours."

"What? I rarely sleep for more than thirty minutes at a time these days. Eight hours?" She sat up, causing the covers to fall and expose her breasts. She jerked her robe closed and glanced to see if he'd been looking.

"Suddenly shy?" he asked. He treated her to a soul scorching smile when she finally dared to look him in the eyes. "How do you feel?"

Thankfully, he didn't press the subject, as she wasn't ready to chat casually about what had happened. And now that he mentioned it, she realized she felt pretty good. Better than she had in weeks. *Odd*. "Better," she said.

"Better than eight hours ago?" he asked with mock shock.

She smiled. She couldn't help it even though she still wasn't ready to talk about it. He was easy to be around. Even in such a screwed-up situation, with him being a prisoner, he managed to tease her and give her the best company she'd had in weeks.

"I'm going to pretend that doesn't hurt my ego," he teased. "Whatcha have to eat around here?"

"Oh, you must be starving. I have a bunch of snacks in the fridge over there." She hopped out of bed, marveling at how steady and energized she felt, grabbed his hand and pulled him behind her to show him the way. She opened the custom-carved wood cabinet that housed a refrigerator. She stepped aside and said, "Help yourself to whatever you want."

"Wow," he said as he looked inside. "Fruit, fruit, and more fruit. Oh and wine, which is made from fruit."

"Oh. Yeah, um, I'm on a fruit diet." Crap, she didn't think about that. *Sempires* derived nourishment from fruit and semen only.

His raised an eyebrow while looking her up and down. "Diet? Looks like you ought to join me for a steak and baked potato."

She knew she looked terrible. She usually didn't dwell on that, but somehow him noticing shamed her.

As her gazed dropped he lifted her chin, "I meant no offense. You're a beautiful woman. I just meant you damn sure don't need to be on a diet."

He called her beautiful. The sincerity in his eyes shocked her. She'd have thought he was only being nice, trying to make her feel good, had she not seen his eyes. The knowledge shot warm sensations through her body.

Dropping his hand from her, he turned back to the fridge and grabbed a large tray of blueberries, bananas, and mangos. He also picked up a bottle of wine. "Why don't you grab a couple glasses and we'll have an indoor picnic."

She smiled at him, liking the sound of a picnic. "Why don't we sit outside?" she suggested.

"I don't think your mother's ready to let me out of this room," he said, frowning.

"No but we can sit on my balcony." At his surprised look, she said, "But don't get any ideas. It's warded. If you try to cross the barrier, the collar will kick in." She felt bad for his predicament. It certainly wasn't fair to him. "I'm really sorry about all this."

He gave her a look she didn't quite understand, then agreed. "The balcony it is. Uh, where is it?"

She grabbed two wine glasses and a corkscrew off a shelf next to the refrigerator, then opened a large dresser and pulled out a green towel and tossed it to him. "I think it's big enough to fit around your waist."

He caught it and treated her to a charming smile.

"What?" he asked. "Don't like the view?"

"The view is..." *Too damn tempting*. "Well, I thought you might like to cover up. It's all I have to offer you unless you can squeeze into one of my robes."

He eyed her wardrobe as if considering it, then shook his head. "No. A little too feminine for me. It's definitely working for you though."

She flushed at his appreciative gaze.

He wrapped the towel around his waist and knotted it at one side. It didn't make the sight of him any less desirable as she'd hoped. He posed a threat to her resolve. She should be keeping her distance rather than planning a picnic.

She motioned to the far end of the room. "Over there. Follow me."

He followed her through the archway at the end of the room and then through a small door that opened to an expansive stone balcony. A white, wrought-iron table and two chairs sat in the middle of the balcony. Plants adorned matching, multi-tiered wrought-iron stands on each side of the balcony.

He placed the fruit tray on the table and opened the wine. She held the glasses as he poured.

She took a seat and popped a blueberry into her mouth, closing her eyes as she savored the taste. She forced herself to eat a little every day, but the flavors had eluded her since she'd begun weakening. She didn't know why she felt so much better today, but she wanted to enjoy it while she could.

She took a sip of wine and sighed. Damn that tasted good. Sweet and fruity, flowing down her throat, warming her. She took a larger sip. Then another. So good.

When she opened her eyes, Kean sat across from her, staring. "What's wrong?" she asked, feeling self-conscious.

"Just watching you enjoy the wine," he said.

She smiled and popped a blueberry into her mouth. "It's been a while since it actually tasted good to me. I don't mean to be a lush."

"Don't sensor yourself on my account. Other than bringing out the lush in you," he winked at her, "I can tell you feel better. I'm glad."

"Me too. Maybe I'm in a remission of sorts."

He took a long draw from his wine glass, swallowed and refilled both their glasses. "Tell me what's happening to you."

She looked away and sighed, "I don't want to bore you."

"Wouldn't ask if I thought it would." he teased.

"Funny." She looked at the sky, considering how much she could share with him. "I have a *condition*. I suppose you could say a nutritional imbalance." Giggling, she took another big swig from her glass.

"That doesn't sound so serious," he offered. "Eat what you're missing or take some vitamins."

To change the subject, she abruptly asked, "Where do you live? What do you do? Do you have family?" Oh god. She hadn't thought of that when she'd brazenly accepted his offer to pleasure her. *Please don't let him have a wife and kids at home.* She'd never forgive herself, and she'd be forced to despise him. She didn't want to despise him. He was so likeable. *And hot.*

He grinned at her. "Not a very subtle change of subject but I'll play. I live in Texas. My father and grandfather are living. My mother passed away twenty years ago." He paused and looked sheepish as he continued. "I don't do anything in the way of working, if that's what you meant. My family has acquired great wealth that's been passed down through the generations. With smart investments, the money grows so there's no need for working. I do volunteer my time for rebuilding and cleanup efforts after hurricanes, oil spills—that sort of thing."

She had to smile at that. With his wealth, he could be a totally spoiled, self-centered individual, but he chose to help people in need.

"That's really nice of you. I think I'd like to do something like that," she said.

He treated her to a breathtaking smile and said, "You should join me sometime."

Both of their smiles faltered and an awkward silence followed. What were either of them thinking? She'd be dead soon and even if she wasn't, they'd certainly never see each other again after this. Dead soon. That sounded so foreign to her at the moment, sitting there with Kean, picnicking and enjoying each other's company. The undeniable attraction blazing between them. She felt as if they were on a date rather than imprisoned together, and she wanted it to last. If only...

She took another large gulp of her wine and then held her glass out for him to refill it. It tasted so damn good and made her feel all warm and bubbly. She watched him pop a banana slice in his mouth and guessed it wasn't all that satisfying for a hungry man.

She wanted to do something nice for him—a small effort to show her appreciation of his company—forced or not. She couldn't remember the last time she'd enjoyed herself so much.

"Hey, stay here, I'll be right back," she said as she went inside.

When she returned, he stood looking over the balcony.

"Thinking about jumping?" she joked. At least, she hoped he wasn't thinking about that.

He turned to her. "No, just looking at the scenery. Lotta trees."

"Fruit trees," she said. She grabbed her wine glass, topped it off, and joined him at the balcony ledge. "There are several acres of them on our land. Almost any kind of fruit you can think of is being grown here. My favorites are mangoes and blueberries. Before I weakened, I loved helping the gardeners pick the fruit."

"Where exactly are we? The air is thick. And the sky is hazy around the perimeter of all those trees. It's like the sun isn't shining beyond the orchard." He frowned.

"I'm no gardener, but don't different types of fruits need different climates?"

Crap. They were in the veil between the human realm and the demon realm, but she couldn't tell him that. And he was right. The air in the veil was thick and the sky hazy. For a price, certain things in the veil, such as plants and trees and light, could be manipulated by elemental demons. Beyond their plot of space, in the veil, there was nothing—just a vast, hazy barrier that separated the human realm from the demon realm. Until, of course, you came across another occupied plot.

"Okay, if you can't answer the where, tell me more about this *nutritional imbalance* and why you can't simply eat differently," he suggested.

She sighed then hiccupped. She enjoyed the easy conversation between them and wished she didn't have to be secretive.

"Well, Kean. Lemme tell you. I don't want to *eat* what is required to *fix* my *issue*. It'll turn me into something I don't want to be. I'll be overcome by needs, desires." She gulped the rest of her wine.

Her mother and sister refused to understand. She wanted to talk to someone who might and Kean seemed genuinely interested. Hell, why not tell him? It might be fun and he'd, of course, not believe a word of it anyway.

Plus, as she held onto the balcony ledge for support, she realized she was quite buzzed.

"You definitely have my attention," he said.

"If you think that's good stuff, listen to this. My need is semen, as my mother told you. I am what is called a *Sempire*. Kinda like a vampire, I suppose. But instead of blood, I need semen to survive. Hence the reason you are locked up with me. My mother wants you to give me your semen because that's the only thing that will *fix* my *condition*. How'dya like that?"

Instead of freaking out, calling her crazy, or laughing in her face, he simply asked, "Why do you refuse what will fix your condition?"

She stared at him, dumbfounded and swayed as she stepped to the table to grab the bottle of wine. Empty. Damn it. "I'll be back," she slurred.

Kean grasped her shoulders, steadying her. "Have a seat. I'll grab another bottle."

She plopped onto the chair. "Good idea. Thanks."

He returned quickly and refilled her glass. "You were about to tell me why you refuse what you need," he prompted.

"I don't want to be a whore. I don't want to be forced to go from man to man to get what I need to survive."

Kean seemed to consider her words. "Wouldn't one man be able to sustain you?"

She snorted. "It doesn't seem to sustain my mother and sister. But, they don't care. They are full-blooded and until I feed I am a half-breed. Being half-human, I'd hoped the human half would win and the *Sempire* needs wouldn't control me. My refusal to give in is what's killing me. Once I do give in, it's all over. I'll transform to full *Sempire*, the needs will kick in completely, and I'll become everything I've fought so hard to avoid."

"Half human?" Kean asked.

She nodded. "Yep, that's right. My mother tells me that's where my silly notion of a monogamous relationship comes from—my human half. Is it really that silly? What if I meet someone and fall in love and then he is unavailable to me for a few of days? I'd be forced to—to—" she scrunched her face in disgust, "cheat."

She couldn't believe she spewed all that information to a human, but it felt great to purge, and she had to swallow the hysterical laughter building inside her. Kean must think her totally insane but was considerate enough to not let on.

"I see your dilemma," Kean said.

KEAN COULDN'T BELIEVE the change in her. Couldn't believe what he was hearing. She was half human and willing to let herself die because she might fall in love and might be forced to cheat on that person. Shit, her whole attitude toward her *Sempire* half would probably change if she'd simply give in to her needs.

He never thought he'd meet a *Sempire*, and certainly didn't expect her to be innocent if he did. He liked her and didn't like the idea of her dying. He also felt like a fucking asshole for what he'd done to her as she slept now that he knew her reasons. Who'd have thought? A *romantic Sempire*?

He wondered if the little bit of semen he'd passed to her was enough to make the change in her she'd mentioned. It had certainly strengthened her. Hell, she was sitting there getting drunk with him and telling him, who she thought was human, that she was a semen-reliant demon.

He chuckled silently to himself. Yeah, he definitely liked her. She had spunk. If she'd embrace her nature, they could be friends, hang out and cruise clubs for sexual conquests. Maybe have a foursome. Odd, that idea suddenly annoyed him.

"Araya?" A male voice called.

"Oh, thanks, Fin. Will you set it here?" She motioned to the table.

A thirty-ish, muscular male wearing a tight grey t-shirt and jeans carried a dome-covered platter and set it on the table in front of Kean. He sensed demon in the male but couldn't make out what type.

"What's this?" Kean asked.

"This is your dinner." She smiled as Fin lifted the dome, revealing a huge, juicy steak and a large baked potato.

"Holy shit. This looks great," Kean exclaimed.

"Anything else?" Fin asked.

Kean shook his head, but Fin stood staring at Kean as if waiting for something more. "Thanks, this should do it," Kean said. He hoped the guy wasn't waiting for a tip, because obviously he didn't have a wallet on him. *Hello, I'm naked except for a towel.*

Araya stood and hugged Fin. "Thanks for getting that ready so fast."

He finally looked away from Kean, hugged Araya back and said, "No problem. I aim to please. How are you feeling? You look different."

"A little tipsy," Araya answered. "But seriously, much better today. Must be the solid sleep I had."

"Good to hear," Fin said, sounding genuinely relieved. "See you later." He winked at her, gave Kean one last strange look, and walked away.

What was that guy's problem? Did he have a thing for Araya?

"Is that one of your lovers?" Kean growled, his mood darkening.

Araya looked surprised. "Fin? Fin is our chef and a good friend. He's lived here since before I was born." The corners of her mouth turned down. "I thought you'd enjoy the steak and potato you mentioned earlier."

What the hell was his problem? His good mood instantly changed when Araya hugged Fin and the guy had winked at her. He'd felt like punching the guy who'd just brought him a great looking meal. Being held prisoner must be getting to him.

Araya had done something thoughtful for him, and he'd snapped at her. He shook himself mentally and forced a broad smile. "I'm practically drooling. This is awesome."

There, her smile came back and what a sexy smile it was.

He cut into the steak, forked a piece, and put it in his mouth. He moaned. "Wow. Perfect. You want a piece?"

She scrunched up her face. "Ew, no. I only eat fruit."

"Well," he said after swallowing a bite of potato, "that's your problem. You need some protein."

Her eyes widened as wine spewed from her mouth. He hadn't thought about what he was saying. Hadn't meant it that way. But it cracked him up that she took it that way, and he laughed out loud. Hell, she was laughing too which cracked him up even more.

"Sorry," he said, leaning back in his chair still laughing, "that's not what I meant."

"Oh my god. I must be drunk to laugh at that. Did I get any on you?" she asked as she wiped wine off her foot.

"No, but hey, why do you have a chef and steak on hand if you only eat fruit?" He asked between mouthfuls. That Fin could really cook.

"We tend to have a lot of visitors, such as yourself, in addition to the guards living here."

"What? Your mother abducts a lot of people?"

"Not until recently. Wait, you are the only one she actually kidnapped as far as I know. I still don't understand that. But she and my sister bring a lot of males here. Some stay a day. Sometimes, if they are really *satisfying*, they keep them here for few days or a week. Rarely longer than that."

"I see. Yeah, I suppose most males wouldn't need to be kidnapped for providing those types of services to beautiful women," he agreed.

"No, most don't. Why is it that you don't want to *help* me? I'm curious. The others were more than eager."

"Well, I didn't appreciate being abducted and waking up locked and collared in a cell. Letting someone *force* me to do anything isn't really my style."

"You were locked in a cell? Which one?" she asked, surprise evident on her face.

"You mean there's more than one?" When she nodded, he asked, "Why do you have cells in your basement?"

She shifted awkwardly, selected a slice of mango from the tray, slipped it into her mouth and licked the juice from her lips. He never thought he'd be envious of a piece of fruit until now. He thought she was going to evade his question, but then she spoke.

"That's my mother's business, the family business. Fetish films. That's what the cells are typically used for."

"Wow," Kean said. "Fun family business. Well, maybe not for you," he amended when she didn't share his enthusiasm and decided to bring the subject back to the task at hand.

He paused and looked into her enchanting golden eyes. "I will help you now, if you'll let me," he said in a low, husky tone.

She drew in a deep breath, the intensity of her gaze as it met his made his cock twitch. Yeah, he didn't only want to help her to gain his freedom, he wanted to pleasure her again and then feed his shaft into that sultry mouth of hers. He wanted to be the one to strengthen her. He wanted to feel the ecstasy of filling her mouth and nourishing her with his essence as he watched her come alive because of it.

Her gaze fell to his lap. Yep, she noticed his lengthening cock tenting the towel. She took another sip of wine and licked her lips.

Bringing her eyes back to his her tone turned husky. "Why are you offering now?"

"Technically, this is my second offer," he reminded her. "I changed my mind when I caught you watching me in the shower."

She chewed her lower lip as her eyes shifted to his lap once again. "Please don't," she breathed. "I told you why. I don't want that kind of life." Tears threatened to spill from her eyes. He didn't like it.

"Hey," he said, purposefully forcing a cheerful tone, "no problem. Just thought I'd offer." He picked up a blueberry. "Open your mouth."

Her eyes bugged. "What?"

"Let's see if I can make it," he said playfully.

Understanding, she brushed the back of her hand over her eyes, wiped away the moisture, and opened her mouth.

He tossed it right in. She laughed and said, "My turn." She chose a piece of banana and tossed it, but it hit him square in the nose.

"Ug, you throw like a girl," he chuckled as he pulled the banana off his nose.

Shrugging, she popped some fruit in her mouth and washed it down with the rest of her wine.

"More?" he asked, indicating the wine bottle.

"I think I've had more than enough." She picked up her glass and tipped it toward him. "So why not have one more?"

"I like your style," he said as he filled her glass.

"So, my mother approached you and asked you to leave with her and you refused?" Araya asked.

"No. She approached, introduced herself, and I followed her outside. That's the last thing I remember before waking up in the cell."

Araya frowned. "I don't understand that. Usually all she has to do is ask. I mean, you've seen her, she's perfect. I wonder why she didn't present the option to you. If you didn't agree, she could've approached someone else."

Kean no longer agreed about Talith's perfection since experiencing her personality. He'd take Araya's company over hers any day. Kean hadn't really thought about it much, but Araya was right. If Talith had simply asked the other men she'd brought home for Araya, why hadn't she asked him? Why had he been important enough to kidnap?

Was it possible? Surely not. If Talith knew Kean was part Incubus, she'd either have avoided him or killed him. She couldn't possibly *want* an Incubus locked in a room with her *Sempire* daughter. She couldn't possibly *want* her daughter to become addicted to his semen. Or could she? Maybe she was desperate enough to save her daughter she'd do it regardless of possible consequences.

Kean wanted to help Araya now, and he would if she'd agree to it, but he feared she would become addicted. If that happened, she'd end up dying anyway. No one else's semen would work for her once addiction set in. Being only an eighth Incubus, it was doubtful she'd become addicted, but hell he didn't know one way or the other. He needed to talk to Talith and feel her out.

Kean jumped to his feet as a bone-rattling screech pierced his eardrums. Something large and winged flew right toward Araya. It wasn't a bird, that was for damn sure. And it looked mean and hungry. He immediately dove and knocked Araya to the ground falling on top of her. He didn't have time to wonder about his instinct to protect her.

In the next moment, he was dragged off her and flipped over. Orange eyes glared at him from a large, blue-black, furry head. The thick, elongated snout sniffed him, and its mouth opened revealing a full set of pointy teeth. The things' wings spanned four feet. *What the fuck?*

"Kiberry, no!" Araya yelled.

Kiberry?

The beastly creature gave Kean one last sniff then sauntered to Araya, wagged its short, furry tail, and licked her face. Its wings retracted into its sides. She giggled and gave it a hug.

"Where have you been? I haven't seen you in weeks," she said to it. It lay down and rolled onto its back, its tiny legs straight up in the air. Araya rubbed its belly, and the thing made a rumbling noise he assumed was a sound of approval.

"What the hell is *that*?" Kean asked.

"This is Kiberry. He's a baby *Tengur*. My sister and I found him hiding in the orchard. We don't know what happened to his mother, but he took to us. He's our buddy."

"A Teng-what? And *that's* a *baby*?" he asked. He'd never seen such a thing.

She laughed, still rubbing the beast's belly. "A *Tengur*. And yes. He's only a year and a half old. They usually stay with their mothers until two years of age. So technically, he's still a baby."

"You have seen its teeth right?" he asked, wondering if she was oblivious to the danger.

"Yes. He's capable of doing damage for sure, but as long as he likes you, you're in no danger. He wouldn't leave my or Valia's side for the first few months after taking him in. He saw that we favored kiwi fruit and blueberries so he ate them too. Hence the name, Kiberry."

"Cute. A little too cute. I swear it wanted to eat me."

"*He* not *it,*" she corrected him. You might be right. He's protective of us. When he saw you tackle me, he probably thought you were trying to hurt me."

"Shit. I thought *I* was protecting you," Kean explained. "I've never seen anything like *him* before. Can you blame me?"

Araya stood and Kiberry followed her lead. "You two should meet properly," she said as she led the beast to where he stood. It took all of his will power to stand his ground. Kean never shied away from a fight. He was no pussy, but he'd never faced a fucking winged monster demon before.

"Kiberry, this is Kean. He's a friend. Shake his hand," Araya said.

Was she serious? Kiberry stood on his four-inch-long back legs and held out a front paw-claw to Kean. Kean extended his hand so as not to insult Araya or the beast, but he wasn't all that crazy about it. Kiberry's claws wrapped around Kean's hand and thankfully didn't rip the skin from his bones.

"Kiberry, can Kean pet your head?" she asked.

"That's okay," Kean said quickly. "A handshake is good."

Kiberry dropped to all fours and head-butted Kean's leg. Kean looked to Araya and she nodded for him to go ahead. Kean leaned down and stroked the top of the beast's head. The softness of the fur surprised him.

"Okay. Now you don't have to worry about him eating you," she teased. "Now that's settled, I'm thinking I need to lie down."

"Feeling bad?" he asked, truly concerned.

"Not really bad, a little woozy from the wine and tired. Maybe I overdid it. This is the most energetic I've been in months."

She strolled ahead of him, back to the room, the beast following close behind her. He noticed her sway a little and he chuckled silently when she held her arms out to steady herself as if she were taking a drunk test.

She plopped onto the bed and wrapped the covers around her. The beast spread his wings and flapped them once, lifting him high enough to reach the top of the bed. It tucked its wings in, turned around in a circle and curled into Araya's side. She absently stroked its head. "I'm afraid I'm about to pass out," she said. Regret stained her words.

"That's okay. I'll entertain myself."

Her eyes fluttered closed, her voice soft and small, "Kean?"

"Yeah?"

"I enjoyed our picnic tonight," she said without opening her eyes.

"Me too," he said. He meant it too. He'd enjoyed her company and wished she had enough energy to stay awake and spend more time with him.

"Kean?" She called to him again.

"Yeah?"

"My bed is huge. You don't have to sleep in a chair."

Oh how he wished that was an invitation for more, but he recognized it for what it was. She was simply being nice. "You already have a bed buddy."

"There's still plenty of room. He really won't hurt you."

"Okay. Sleep well."

Kean waited for Araya to drift off before striding to the intercom at the far end of the room. He pressed the "call" button.

A male voice answered almost immediately. "Yes?"

"I need to speak with Talith. Now. Privately."

"I'll inform her of your request."

The door to Araya's room opened five minutes after he told the voice on the intercom he wanted to see Talith. She didn't even glance at him as she made her way to Araya's bed. She looked at her daughter, then turned to him and crooked a finger for him to follow.

A guard stood outside the room.

"She looks better," Talith said, "but she hasn't submitted completely. She'd have more color in her face and more energy if she had. What did you do?"

Kean shifted uncomfortably and avoided answering. "I'd like to talk to you," he looked down at the towel that barely wrapped around his waist, "privately and preferably with some clothes on."

Talith stared at him for a long moment then nodded to the guard. "Balcony."

The guard disappeared ahead of them and Talith said, "Follow me."

By the time they arrived at the end of the long hallway, the guard had reappeared. He handed Kean a blue robe. He shrugged into it and belted it around his waist. *Comfy*.

"You stay here," Talith said to the guard as she opened the door leading to a balcony off the opposite side of the mansion.

They sat across from one another on wrought-iron chairs similar to those where he and Araya had picnicked.

"What's on your mind?" Talith asked.

Kean didn't really have a plan and picked his words carefully. "After talking to Araya tonight, I found out there have been others in my current *position*. However, I'm the only one who was not given a choice about being here. Why is that?"

Talith leaned back in her chair, her cool expression didn't falter. "Perhaps I was tired of asking and decided to simplify the process."

"I don't think so. Why would you waste your time on someone who might not be interested? Had you asked and I refused, you could have simply moved on to someone else. Why me?"

This time, her composure slipped a bit but only for a moment. "What are you getting at?"

He leaned forward, no longer intimidated by his situation or the fact that he knew she could kill him or have him killed easily. "I think you know what I'm getting at."

"Perhaps I do," she said. "Perhaps you shouldn't concern yourself with it."

"What?" Kean couldn't believe she'd said that. "I'm a prisoner here and I shouldn't concern myself with it?"

"I will do what I have to do to save my daughter. If you are inconvenienced in the process, that's too goddamn bad," Talith spat at him and her eyes turned black.

Okay. That bitch was scary when she got angry. He still wasn't ready to come out in case she didn't actually know what he was so he said, "How inconvenienced will your daughter be if—" he stopped to regroup but there was no need. Talith already caught his drift confirming his suspicion was right.

"My hope is that Araya will be fine once you've left. Considering your *deficit* it's my assumption the effect will not be long lasting if there is any effect at all."

His deficit? What a bitch. She locked her daughter in a room, imprisoned him and now he knew she was willing to risk addicting her daughter to him. She knew he was part Incubus. She fucking knew and that was why she chose him, didn't give him an option. It had to be him to tempt Araya more than any other could. Well, a full-blooded Incubus would tempt her more, but would definitely be too dangerous. Deficit? He'd show her his deficit. "And if you're wrong? If she isn't fine?"

"Then," her eyes glittered angrily, "you'll be staying with us for a very long time, *mixed-breed.*"

Holy fuck. She'd keep him here. Keep him a prisoner forever if necessary. Kean had to find a way out of this mess, but he didn't want to hurt Araya. If he could get her to submit fully to him once, the danger to her should be minimal—hopefully—and she should strengthen significantly, allowing him to get out of here. He needed an edge. She'd obviously been tempted by him but not enough to give in.

"Since we aren't playing games anymore, why don't you arm me with some info? Where's the weakness? Where's my advantage?" he asked.

Talith looked thoughtful. "Our kind can scent semen as if it were a cologne freshly spritzed on your skin. The more aroused you become, the more fragrant and alluring the scent. Even with your deficit, *your* scent is tantalizing because of the Incubus blood coursing through your veins." She inhaled deeply and her pupils dilated slightly.

That's why Araya had been so focused on him in the shower. Why she'd been drawn to him and so aroused she'd let him touch her. He understood about tantalizing scents. When Araya was aroused, her smell intoxicated him. Yes, he could use this information to his advantage.

"I'll need a way to keep your daughter from running or hiding from me," he said, a plan forming in his mind.

"We've been over this, you cannot force her," Talith warned.

"I wouldn't *force* her to do anything but stay in one place so she can't avoid me."

Talith tapped a slender forefinger against her lips. "Ah, I believe I get your drift. Walk with me."

Talith whispered to the guard as they left the balcony and entered the house. He strode ahead of them while Kean and Talith made their way back to Araya's room. The guard appeared a few seconds later and handed Kean two silk scarves.

Talith said, "In her weakened condition, these should be sufficient."

"Will the collar see this as me trying to hurt her?" he asked.

"Only if your intent *is* to hurt her."

"Wait," Kean said, "one more request. Can you get that beast out of her bed?"

Talith's eyes narrowed. "Beast?"

"The furry one with wings," he explained.

"Oh, Kiberry?" She laughed at him but opened the door, made a *psst* sound and patted her leg. The beast stood, walked to the edge of the bed, spread its wings and floated to the floor. Kean would swear it looked at him disdainfully as it walked past him into the hallway.

"Good luck mixed-breed," Talith said and closed the door.

Chapter Four

Kean padded to the bed where Araya still slept. Her cheeks already looked slack again and her face had lost most of its earlier glow.

He dropped the robe, surprised Talith hadn't stripped him of it before locking him back in the room. He supposed she didn't think it necessary considering he'd decided to do what she wanted him to do.

Kean tried not to think of how pissed Araya would be when she woke up, and he tried to tell himself he didn't care anyway. He had a life to get back to and this seemed the only way to do it. Besides, he would be saving her life, and she might end up thanking him in the long run.

He gently wrapped one silk scarf around her wrist. When she didn't stir, he carefully lifted her wrist above her head and tied the loose end of the scarf to the bedpost. She grumbled and he froze but she didn't wake. He repeated the process with her other wrist.

Kean's cock hardened from the mere possibility of Araya watching him, desiring him. The thought that he'd be the only one she hadn't turned away stroked his ego.

He sat on the bed looking at her, imagining how her mouth would feel wrapped around his cock. How her nipples would bead while she sucked him. He'd penetrate her mouth, pumping into its slickness while she sucked and lapped at him. How her delicious cunt would flood in anticipation of him fucking her. Yeah, he wanted her to want him.

He gripped his shaft and stroked it. Pre-come had already formed at the tip. He ran his fingers over the head on the upstroke and massaged it downward. He imagined it was her wetness coating his cock.

Araya stirred, her breathing becoming irregular.

He stroked her cheek with his free hand. "Araya," he said softly and her eyes fluttered open.

"What? What are you doing?" She cried out. She struggled to move but realized her hands were tied. "Untie me!" She shrieked.

"I'm saving us both," Kean said, his voice raw.

"You traitor! I thought you understood. You've been working against me the whole time," she accused as she struggled against her bonds.

The betrayal in her eyes stung him. But he had a mission. To save her. To save himself. He wouldn't be deterred no matter how much like a cocksucker he felt.

"It won't work. I won't let it." She squeezed her eyes shut.

"Araya, look at me. I'm hard for you. *This* is for you."

Eyes still closed, she pleaded, "Please stop, Kean. I don't want this."

He hesitated. The pleading tone in her voice cut him. But what the hell was he supposed to do? Being a prisoner didn't work for him, and she still had the option to say no. It was her choice even if what he was doing made it difficult for her.

Her breathing deepened, and her nipples peaked beneath her thin robe. What he'd give to suck them into his mouth, tickle them with his tongue. To lick her sweet cunt until she screamed his name in ecstasy.

"Thinking of touching you, pleasing you, is driving me crazy. I'm getting close, Araya."

Her eyes popped open. She licked her lips as she watched him pump his cock. Faster now. Her eyes followed his movements, and he groaned as she licked her lips.

"Do you want to taste me, Araya?"

"Noooo," she whined. Her dilated pupils gave away the lie.

More droplets of pre-come oozed from the tip of his cock. Araya's eyes bugged and she struggled to free herself from her restraints. He assumed in an effort to flee but then she groaned and said, "I-I need to taste you."

He almost came right then. She was giving in. She wanted him, wanted to taste him. Such sweet words.

The gold in her eyes sparked as her chest heaved from ragged breaths, her gaze never leaving his cock. He moved closer to her, getting on his knees and positioning his cock inches from her face. She looked up at him uncertainly, for a second, then raised her head from the pillow, sticking her tongue out. She touched it to his wet slit and growled a sound of pleasure.

His cock jumped. He was about to fucking explode.

"More," she growled, an unnatural tone hitching her voice. *Sexy as hell.* "Now."

He obliged. No hesitation. He inched closer, giving her full access to his throbbing cock. She latched on with her greedy mouth, and her inexperience didn't lessen his pleasure. Her enthusiasm as she sucked and licked, the scent of her arousal, fruity and seductive—he'd never experienced anything like it.

His slippery cock kept sliding out of her mouth and she growled each time. He figured he could untie her hands now, but she still hadn't actually fed, and she might find the will to stop. So, he braced one hand on the wall and grabbed the base of his cock with the other, holding it steady for her.

She moaned her approval, and his balls clenched at her vigorous slurping. "Araya, I'm—I'm going to come. Are you ready for me?"

She mumbled around his cock and began sucking and licking more vigorously. That was it. She wanted it. She needed it. He couldn't hold it back a second longer.

His hips jerked forward, shoving his cock deeper as semen exploded from him into her eager mouth. The sensation racked his body, his hips thrusting of their own accord as she milked every last drop from him.

His body slumped back to a sitting position, and his dick made a popping sound as it pulled from the stranglehold her lips had on it. She swiped her tongue across her lips, cleaning up every last drop of his release.

Her hair shone and her lips and skin plumped, taking on a rosy glow. The instant transformation was incredible. He'd thought her beautiful before but now stunning, irresistible.

The lust in her eyes struck him as her gaze met his. She'd been fed, but now she needed release, and he'd damn sure give it to her if she'd let him.

"Untie me, Kean," she demanded in a low and husky tone.

He removed one silk tie and then the other. She shook out her arms and commanded him, "Touch me, like you did before."

So damn sexy. "Araya, I want to make you come with my mouth. Like you did for me. Let me lick you. Let me taste your sweetness."

"Yes," she breathed as her legs spread.

He needed no more invitation than that. He dove between her legs, burying his face in her ambrosial scent. Her hips bucked at the assault his tongue waged on her silken folds.

"Oh god, Kean. Feels so good."

He parted her lips with his tongue and delved deep inside, then stroked up and down on her clit. When her knees squeezed together crushing his head, he parted them forcefully with his hands, never stopping the assault on her clit. He sucked. She writhed.

"Yes, oh yes," she wailed as her sweet juices coated his lips and tongue. Warm, sweet, fruity. Pure heaven.

ARAYA'S BODY HUMMED with energy. Oh god. She'd never felt so alive. So hot. And she'd never feasted on anything as exquisite at Kean's cock. She'd almost climaxed when his come had flooded her mouth.

She needed more from him now. Her body craved him, burned for him, demanded an orgasm from him. Only him.

His warm tongue caressing her, probing her—she hadn't known what she was missing. The sensations splitting her insides apart. She grabbed his hair holding him in place, afraid he'd stop the delicious assault his mouth waged on her.

She couldn't bear it. The pleasure, the intensity threatened to make her go mad. Raging waves of bliss blazed through her. Consumed her. Her hips bucked in contrast with the magical swipes of his tongue on her clit.

Her body tensed as white hot sparks shot through her body. She cried out, "Kean. Yes!" as her skin melted and her internal organs turned to mush from the intensity of her climax.

Araya rode the waves of orgasm until she couldn't bear anymore. Her voice was barely a whisper as she pushed at Kean's head. "Stop."

Kean looked up at her a cocky smile splayed his lips. "Sensitive?"

She nodded, too breathless for words.

Kean crawled up the bed and lay next to her on his side propping his head up with one hand. The other hand stroked circles around her stomach, goose bumps trailing in the wake of each stroke.

Kean didn't speak, and she was glad for it. Araya couldn't remember ever feeling so relaxed. Boneless. Content. Somewhere in the back of her mind, she knew she should be royally pissed, but the climax had washed away all coherent thought. Her eyes drifted shut and her mind floated away on a cloud of serenity.

Chapter Five

Araya awoke thinking her bed had never felt warmer and more comfortable than it did right now. She tried to stretch her arms above her head but couldn't. She jerked sideways when she realized Kean's arm was wrapped tight around her. *Oh crap.* The memories slammed into her brain. *Kean. Damn him!*

Araya had successfully avoided her demon nature for almost thirty years. Yeah, she'd have been dead soon, but at least she wouldn't have to face a lifestyle she abhorred. A slave to her cravings, desires. Then he'd come along and screwed it all up. She'd trusted him. Stupid? Obviously. But there had been something about him she'd liked. She enjoyed his company. He was fun and made her laugh.

She'd thought he understood and respected her reasons. But wait, he was a human, so he would have thought she was making up the *Sempire* story anyway. Which meant, there wasn't even anything admirable about what he'd done. He didn't know or believe his semen would actually *fix* her condition, save her. So, he was as bad as the rest of the men. A freaking whore. And he'd made *her* a whore.

Rage overtook her. *Bastard!* She flung Kean's arm off her and punched him square in the face as she jumped from the bed.

He groaned and brought his hand to his cheek. "What the fuck," he yelped.

"You bastard." She stomped to her closet and grabbed a fresh robe, belting it closed dramatically. "You made me like you. I felt sorry for you being here. Kidnapped, my ass. You and my mother planned this out perfectly didn't you? You're probably both so proud of yourselves."

Kean got out of the bed and grabbed a blue robe off the floor. Where the hell had he gotten that? Her mother, no doubt. *Bitch.*

"Araya, I'm sorry." He had the decency to look ashamed. "I decided I didn't like the idea of you dying."

"What?" she shrieked. "You liar. You didn't believe the story I told you. Why would you? You're just like the rest of them. You wanted sex. A blow job.

Whatever. You forced me to do something I didn't want. I hope you're happy with yourself because you make me sick. You have condemned me to a life I don't want."

Kean stormed toward her looking pissed. She tried to take a step back, but he grabbed her by the shoulders. "Araya, I don't have to be locked in a room with a woman and tie her up to get sex. A blowjob. Whatever." He mimicked her words. "I am sorry for your situation. But I didn't force you to do anything. I encouraged you because I wanted to save you and myself.

His voice lowered taking on a seductive tone. "You wanted my cock in your mouth. You asked for a taste and you loved it. Look at what it's done for you. Have you seen yourself? How do you feel?"

It pissed her off that her face burned at his blunt words. It pissed her off more that he was right. Had he held out she would have begged him for a taste. Of course, if he hadn't been masturbating and she hadn't been tied, she wouldn't have been in that situation in the first place.

And she did feel great. She couldn't remember ever feeling so alive and full of energy in her life. She pushed at his chest and he let go of her arms and stepped back.

She stormed to the bathroom and gasped at her reflection in the mirror. Her hair shone as though made of spun silk, her eyes sparkled as if infused by flecks of golden glitter. The dark circles under her eyes had disappeared, and her complexion was young and rosy. She'd never looked so good, not even before she'd begun weakening.

She'd have been excited, in awe, if she didn't know what she had to do to continue feeling and looking so great. But she did know and it stripped away any excitement she might have enjoyed.

She turned away from the mirror and found Kean staring at her from the doorway.

"Amazing transformation, don't ya think?" Kean asked and smiled at her.

"I need you out of my sight. You betrayed me. You used me. You're a whore like the rest. You got what you wanted so just go away."

"Araya," his voice lowered, gentled, "I may qualify as a whore and possibly a betrayer but I did not *use* you. I offered you what you needed and you accepted."

"You say that but there is no way you actually believed your—your," she sputtered, "*semen* would help me. And why aren't you freaking out that it did?"

Kean shrugged. "I knew what you were before you told me. I'm not," he paused and shifted uncomfortably, "I'm not exactly human."

Araya felt her mouth drop open and her eyes bug. "What the hell are you then?"

"You may not like it." She only glared at him until he continued. "I'm an eighth Incubus."

"No. You. Are. Not. My mother wouldn't. She couldn't." Her face burned and not from embarrassment but from pure anger. Her mother surely wouldn't lock her in a room with a freaking Incubus. No way. No freaking way. One thing drilled into a young *Sempire's* brain—stay the hell away from Incubi.

That explained why she scented him so well. Why he smelled so incredibly irresistible. Why she had *needed* to taste him. Couldn't resist. Why even in her anger, the thought of the taste of him, shit, the mere sight of him had her craving more.

It also explained Kiberry's appearance. He never visited her when humans were around. Damn, even Kiberry had sensed the demon in Kean. If only she had, she would have locked herself in the bathroom or shoved him off the balcony. Something, anything to keep him away from her.

Damn her mother. What if she was already addicted to him? She'd be in worse shape than she had been before. At least, if she'd given in to a human, she could move on. But now, now she might be dependent on him. Him only. Forever.

But wasn't that what she wanted? To find one male she could be with? Yeah, she wanted it but she needed love to go with it. Kean didn't love her. He didn't care about saving her either. He wanted to get away from her and did what he had to do to make it happen. What the hell had her mother been thinking bringing a freaking Incubus into their house? Her room?

She pushed past him and stomped to the intercom. She slammed her fist on the button. She didn't wait for the voice on the other end to acknowledge her. As soon as she heard the click, she demanded, "I want to see my mother *right now.*"

TALITH SWEPT INTO THE room ten minutes later, escorted by one of her guards. Her face lit up as she gazed upon Araya. "You look wonderful," Talith exclaimed as she rushed to embrace her daughter.

Araya stepped back and held her hands out keeping her mother at bay.

"You locked me in a room with an Incubus? Do you hate me that much, Mother?"

Talith blanched at Araya's words and shot Kean a look. "Hate you? I love you, dear. I've been trying desperately to save your life."

"By addicting me to an Incubus?" Araya shrieked.

"He's only part Incubus. Weak." Kean growled but Talith continued as if he weren't in the room. "It's highly unlikely you'll develop addiction to him after a few feedings."

Araya felt her face twist in anger. "A few? There will be no more. I want him out of here. Now."

"Dear, look at yourself. Listen to yourself. You are beautiful, strengthened. Fiery. You are a *Sempire* and you've already had sex with him once. Why not again? Was he no good?"

Araya spared Kean a glance. He looked ready to explode.

"I didn't have sex with him," she gritted out.

Her mother looked surprised then smiled. "Ah you... Well, then, good for you, dear. I expected the *mixed-breed* to seduce your virginity from you."

"Don't you dare look pleased. You know how I feel about this. And don't say *mixed-breed* with a sneer. *I'm* a freaking *mixed-breed*."

Talith visibly hardened. "Araya, yes you are half human. But the *Sempire* half will take over mostly wiping out any human in you. We've been over this. It's those uptight human notions that have you wanting love, marriage, monogamy. Once you've fully embraced your demon nature, these things will no longer matter to you. You will accept and thrive on your sexual encounters. You will crave new partners, new semen to energize you."

Araya snorted. "I put up with you locking me in my room and locking men in here with me. It would all have been over soon anyway. But for you to have brought an Incubus to me... What if, mother?"

Talith cut her off. "*If* addiction occurs, then the Incubus stays. Simple as that."

Kean spoke up. "I did what you asked. She's healthy. I won't be a prisoner forever."

Araya wanted to punch him again. *Bastard*. He knew what she was, and he knew the possible complications and he'd done it anyway. But he hadn't been interested at first. Was it possible he wasn't in on it from the beginning? Was it possible he had been kidnapped? It wouldn't change what he'd done but it would make him slightly less of a bastard. *Slightly*.

"How did you find an Incubus?" Araya asked.

"At a nightclub. As I found the other males. Why?" Talith asked.

"So you set out looking for a human and accidentally found an Incubus?" Araya hoped that was the case. It would make her mother slightly less despicable. *Slightly*.

Talith's gaze faltered a second.

"Mother?" Araya demanded.

"If you must know, I'd been searching for an Incubus for a week. What I found was even better. Him. A mixed-breed Incubus. Diluted blood, diluted semen, therefore reducing the risks of addiction but making him much more alluring than any human or other suitable-demon."

"You're evil," Araya spat at her mother.

Talith looked hurt but quickly recovered. "I love you. I have done what needed to be done. I will not apologize for saving my daughter's life." With that she strode from the room. Her guard followed and locked the door behind them.

"I want him out of here." Araya yelled at the closed door. When there was no reply, she stalked to the refrigerator, grabbed a bottle of wine and took it to the balcony, popping the top and drinking directly from the bottle. She couldn't remember ever being so angry in her life.

KEAN FIGURED IT BEST to give Araya some space. What a personality change, and he wasn't ashamed to admit her fiery spunk turned him on. Shit who was he kidding? Everything about his little half-demon turned him on.

Stopping short, he realized she wasn't *his* little half-demon. What was happening to him? He was beginning to think she might be as dangerous to him as he was to her. He really needed to get the fuck outta dodge.

How the hell was he supposed to do that though? Talith wanted them to... Wait. Talith had assumed they'd had sex. Holy shit. It didn't really help his cause but information was information. So, *Sempires* weren't required to ingest semen for it to work its magic on them. No, he couldn't see how that helped him any, but it sure was interesting. Not something he knew.

He hated that Araya was so pissed at him. He hadn't come into this trying to hurt her. Hell, he'd been forced into the situation and had fully intended to hold out. He understood why she'd doubt that though.

Shit. He'd tied her up and jacked off in front of her face. Yeah, no mystery as to why she had the wrong idea.

Hearing the door open, he spun around to see a blazing redhead flounce into the room. Wow. Skin-tight red satin pants hugged her long legs. The shiny black stilettos adorning her feet made her legs look longer. A black sequined halter top barely covered her plump tits and exposed a belly button that sported dangling black and red gems. The extreme red of her hair almost matched the bright pants she wore. Her eyes shone of gold similar to Araya's.

"Whoa!" She exclaimed and eyed him up and down. "No wonder Mom hid you from me and Fin insisted I sneak up here. You are fucking hot." She drew in an exaggerated breath. "And you smell delicious." She frowned then and closed the distance between them, getting right up in his face. She inhaled deeply again. He saw her pupils dilate and he took a step back.

"Your scent is..." Her eyes widened and she jumped back from him. "What are you?"

Shit. Another fucking Sempire to deal with. "I'm Kean. You?"

"That's not what I meant." She pouted. "I'm Valia. Now, *what* are you?"

"Can't you tell?"

To his surprise she burst out laughing and slapped her hands on her thighs. "Mom saddled her daughter with an Incubus? Holy shit. That is *insane.*" After doubling over with laughter she straightened and she said, "Okay, well, that's different. Where's my sister?"

Ah, he should have known by the eyes they were related. The long wavy hair was the same too, only very dramatic differences in color.

"She's getting drunk on the balcony."

"Fantastic. Think I'll join her," she paused and looked at him thoughtfully, "unless you were about to *join* her."

She winked at him. He winked back. "No, I think she'd as soon push me off the balcony as look at me right now."

Valia considered this a moment. "Mom told me Araya was doing well but wouldn't say anything else. She was pretty bitchy. I take it Araya's pissed she gave in. No biggie. She'll get over it soon enough. I can't wait for her to hit the clubs with me."

ARAYA HAD ALREADY DOWNED half the bottle of wine. She stood, looking over the balcony wall, fuming with anger, wishing she had simply jumped over the side and ended it quickly six months ago. But she couldn't do it then and wouldn't do it now.

She spun around as a voice interrupted her rage.

"Holy shit! You are looking H-O-T, girl!" Her sister rushed over to her and spun her around, looking her up and down.

Araya couldn't stop the warmth that spread through her at her sister's appraisal of her. Growing up half-human in a family of full-blooded, stunningly beautiful *Sempires* left her feeling lacking in the looks department. And now, well, she felt beautiful for the first time in her life. Thanks to Kean. *The bastard.*

Her sister jumped up and plopped her butt on the balcony railing. "Tell me all about it," she said excitedly. "Every last detail. He looks and smells yumalicious." Valia's eyes rolled back in her head as she fanned herself with her hand.

Had Araya not been so angry, she might have laughed at her sister's dramatics.

"I don't want to talk about it," Araya said.

Valia pouted. "You're a party pooper. You had an *Incubus*! You *have* to tell me something."

When Araya didn't say anything, Valia said, "Fine. I'll guess." She looked up and tapped her forefinger to her chin as if in deep thought. "Okay. My guess is you got tired of the whole *dying thing*, got on your hands and knees, with your ass in the air and demanded he shove it in your—"

"Stop!" Araya yelled at her sister. "Do you have to be so-so—"

"Totally awesome and imaginative?" Valia asked with a huge grin on her face. "Yes, yes I do. It's a gift. And if you won't tell me, I'll have to keep making things up."

Araya rolled her eyes, but couldn't hold back a laugh any longer. She loved her sister. Deep down she envied her sister's bluntness and her ease with her sexuality. Nothing scared or embarrassed her. And, of course, her beauty was indescribable.

"That's more like it," Valia teased. "You're much more attractive when you laugh. The pissed-off frowny face wasn't working for you. So how'd it happen?"

Araya's entire body heated as images of Kean stroking his magnificent cock filled her mind. She gave her sister the much abbreviated version of the story.

"Wow. I understand why you couldn't resist suck—" she tamed her words when Araya shifted awkwardly, "gave in to him. I started drooling after getting a whiff of him."

Araya growled. Thinking of her sister drooling over Kean had her ready to shove her sister off the balcony. Her gut had instantly tensed and she'd had to forcibly restrain herself.

"Whoa," Valia said. "Down girl. I only sniffed him. No touching. However, he's so hot, if you don't want him, I'd be glad to borrow him—"

Before Araya knew what the hell she was doing, she grabbed her sister by the hair and pulled her to her feet, her other hand balled into a fist. Valia, being a fully transformed *Sempire*, had always been much stronger than Araya. She still was but Araya could feel her own strength increasing since feeding on Kean. Valia blocked Araya's punch and held her at arm's length, the grin never leaving her face.

"Yep, you got it bad. So, is this fierce possessiveness love, lust, or addiction?" She didn't give Araya a chance to answer. "Knowing you, I'd bet on love." She crinkled her face in mock disgust.

"I don't love him. I hardly even know him," she denied.

"Well, maybe it's a little of all three. Are you calm enough for me to let go? I can't have you marring my awesomeness."

Araya realized she had been about to hit her sister. Why the hell did she care if her sister *borrowed* Kean? For all she cared, Valia could have him. Araya wanted him out of her room. Out of her life. He'd doomed her to being the whore she never wanted to be. So why did those thoughts make her insides wince? What if her mother was wrong? What if she was already reliant on him?

Valia released her and handed her the bottle of wine she must have set down before attacking. "Drink up. Hopefully it'll improve your attitude. Although, I kind of like you feisty like this. It's great to see some life in you."

Araya stumbled to the wrought-iron table and fell into the seat next to it. Addicted to an Incubus. An eighth Incubus. What would she do now? She couldn't let her mother hold him as a prisoner. He didn't deserve that even though he qualified as a first-class bastard. She was back to square-one she supposed. Denying the one thing that would keep her alive. But if her mother knew, she'd never let Kean go. No matter what. She couldn't let her know.

"Valia, don't tell Mother about my outburst, okay?" Araya asked.

Valia snorted. "Of course not. None of her business. But why?"

"I want her to let Kean go, if she thinks I'm addicted, she won't."

Valia pursed her pink lips. "But if you are, you'll need him. I don't want you to suffer anymore. Especially not after seeing your transformation."

"Please Valia. He's only an eighth. Even Mother told me the chances of that were slim with his diluted semen."

Valia looked thoughtful for a moment. "Yeah, that's true. Maybe mild withdrawals but nothing major. Okay. I'm in as long as you promise to take care of yourself from now on. I'm so excited for us to go out cruising for..."

Araya's mind wandered as her sister blathered on and on about picking up males. She had to talk her mother into letting Kean go. If she wasn't already dependent on him she would be after a few more feedings. She knew she'd not be able to resist for long with him in such close proximity and after experiencing such amazing pleasure at his skilled hands. Her mother wanted her to *feed* from him *a few times* though. Damn her.

She didn't see any way around it. She had no clue how to remove the collar from Kean's neck, and he couldn't leave with it on. She'd have to do it. She'd have to feed from him one more time. Surely her mother would accept twice. Once with him had had such a dramatic effect on her, twice should be good enough. She'd convince her mother she'd converted and couldn't wait to get on with the rest of her *Sempire* life.

KEAN SAT. WAITING. Waiting for Araya and her sister to finish gossiping or whatever it was females did. He'd given her space for as long as he could stand it and he needed to make her believe he hadn't intended to trick her. Most importantly that he hadn't used her. He didn't like her anger directed at him. The hurt in her eyes gnawed at his guts. And he didn't fucking know why.

"I think she likes you, Incubus," Valia announced as she flounced past him toward the door. Before leaving, she hesitated and turned back to him. "Thank you for saving my sister. Now we can go out and find hot males together. I actually have a *Ferox* demon in mind for her. Never had one myself, but heard they're wild and scrumptious."

Kean's fists clenched at his sides. A growl rumbled from deep within. He knew of *Ferox* demons. They were huge and wild and embodied the whorish nature Araya despised. Okay. So maybe he did too but the thought of her with *that* disgusted him. Kean would please her. Give her what she needed. A *Ferox* demon would fuck her like an animal and walk away.

Valia's laugh broke through his thoughts. "I like you, Incubus." She winked at him and left the room.

What the hell was that about? He'd never understand females. Outside the bedroom anyway.

Araya walked into the room. His male ego bolstered at the sight of her—knowing he was responsible for her transformation into the sensuous beauty that walked toward him now. His cock instantly hardened as she dropped her robe and stood before him naked. But she'd turned him on even before, when she'd been weak. Yeah, it didn't matter with this female. She turned his crank either way.

"What are you doing?" Kean asked, surprised.

"What I need to do to get you out of here. Out of my life." She dropped to her knees and parted his robe.

"What the fuck? What's that supposed to mean?" Kean grabbed her arms at the shoulders and pulled her until she stood.

"Just let me do this. Satisfy my mother. And she'll let you go. We'll both get what we want."

Kean couldn't believe his ears. She hated him so much she'd do this willingly but apparently with no feeling so she could get rid of him faster. He was hard and ready for her, yes. But he didn't want her unless she wanted him, wanted him as desperately as she had last night.

"Araya, I don't want you like this," he said softly.

Her eyes narrowed and her face flushed. "You're rejecting me *now*?"

"I mean that I don't want you unless you want me. I don't want you to lower yourself and do something you don't desire simply because you're angry," he explained.

"What?" She squealed. "You won't have me now but you forced," his fingers dug painfully into her shoulders so she amended, "you *tricked* me into it before."

His face hardened. "I offered. You accepted. You truly desired me at that time. We've been over this already."

"Damn you." The words left Araya's mouth as a hiss.

He watched her inhale deeply and saw her pupils dilate with every breath, the gold flecks in her eyes sparkling brighter. She reached up and gently but firmly pushed his hands from her arms and stepped up to him on tiptoes, her lips less than an inch from his.

"Can't you tell? Don't you know?" She breathed against his lips. "I hate you for what you've done but I do want you. I can't *not* want you."

Music to his fucking ears. Her scent engulfed him. Damn right she wanted him and he'd give her what she needed, what she desired. He'd give her an experience to remember, to cherish even if she hated him. He'd make sure she felt loved her first time. Make sure she felt treasured so she had a memory to hold onto if she ever felt like a whore for doing what she'd be compelled to do from now on.

Thinking of her hopping from male to male enraged him. Knowing it was his fault overwhelmed him with guilt. But he'd saved her life, right? That had to count for something.

He stroked her cheek with his fingers. He moved forward and inclined his head until his lips barely brushed hers, her fruity breath warming his lips. "You hate me now and you'll hate me more tomorrow, but tonight, I want you to use me. Pretend I'm the only one you'll ever desire. Pretend you love me, Araya. Let me be your *one*, your fantasy."

Their lips met and she threw her arms around his neck following his lead, matching every thrust of his tongue with abandon. Her body molded to his, fitting him perfectly. He wanted to go slow and be gentle and loving. He'd have to reign himself in to accomplish that feat if her kisses alone made him this hot. His cock, already hard, ached with a need to fill her. His desire to spread her and plunge into her depths, give her every last inch of him, burned within him.

He lifted her and she wrapped her legs around him as he carried her to the bed. He only broke the kiss when he sat her down then slid his hands under the shoulders of her robe making it fall from her body. He quickly discarded his robe. As soon as it hit the floor Araya groaned, grasped his shaft and wrapped her sultry lips around the head of his cock before he knew her intent. His knees buckled at the incredible sensation, but that's not what this time was about. He struggled to gain control and pulled out of her delicious hold.

"No," Kean croaked. "I'll spill too soon if you touch me like that." He kneeled on the floor between her legs. "I want to give you what you want if only for one night. Pretend with me. Let the illusion take over. I'll make love to you if you'll have me."

"Make love," she echoed his words. "I'll never have that." The sadness in her tone was unmistakable.

"Let me give that to you now," he urged.

She studied him through heavily lidded eyes, lust and regret burning brightly within their depths.

"Yes," she agreed, "pretend with me tonight."

"Lie back, Araya. I need to taste you now. I can't resist another second."

She obeyed and lay back on the bed with her legs bent at the knees hanging over the edge of the bed. Goddamn she was sexy. Her golden curls couldn't hide the moisture coating her enticing cunt. Her sharp intake of breath spurred him on as he slowly licked from bottom to top, lingering at her clit. She was already so swollen, so ready for him. *Control yourself.*

His tongue lashed her engorged clit with vigor, her nectarous taste and her enthusiasm driving him mad with lust. Her hips bucked as she fisted the sheets.

"Kean. Please, I want it, you, I..." she stuttered between strangled gasps.

Watching her expression of ecstasy blew him away. So untamed. He'd never been as intrigued and turned on by any of his other sexual encounters. This female—this demon—sunk her claws into him and pricked all the right nerves.

"Not yet," he said against her clit. "I want your sweet cunt to weep with desire for me, Araya. I want you to desire me like you'll never desire another," he said as he plunged his tongue inside her slick opening.

"Oh god," she wailed, thrusting her hips, making his tongue go deeper. "I do. Please," she panted. "I want..."

"Tell me," he encouraged her. "Tell me what you want and I'll give it to you."

"I want to feel you. Need to know..."

He drew her clit into his mouth, rolling his tongue slowly over the engorged bud. He wanted her to want him like no other, wanted to know, without a doubt, she wouldn't be able to say he tricked her into this. The fantasy didn't work unless she was mindless with lust and emotion for him.

"Do you want me to lick you until you come?" he asked as he inserted a finger inside her. She gasped. "Or do you want something else? Something more than this?"

"Yes," she answered breathlessly.

He chuckled, deep and throaty. "Which one? You can't have both at the same time. Choose."

She thrust against his finger, her chest heaving from ragged breaths. He'd do whatever she wanted but damn he wanted to hear her say it. Wanted to hear her beg him to slide his hard cock inside her.

And damn did he want to know the feel of being inside her slick depths. Wanted to know it with a desperation that made his cock ache.

Her lust-filled eyes opened halfway as she gazed at him, still thrusting against his finger.

"I want..." she moaned as he swiped his tongue across her clit. I want you to make love to me. Be my *one*, Kean. Show me how it feels to be loved."

Her words made his heart hitch and his cock jump as his balls pulled tight against his body. Perfect. He rose from the floor and pulled her to her feet, wrapping his arms around her, pulling her body into his as their lips met in an urgent but gentle kiss.

"Please," she breathed against his lips.

"Yes, I'll make love to you, Araya. I want nothing more in this moment."

He laid her back on the bed and hooked her legs over his forearms. He spread her wide and settled between her legs. He gripped his shaft and ran the head of his cock up and down between her flooded lips. Her eyes rolled back into her head as he pressed into her drenched cunt. Slowly. Inch by torturous inch. Fuck. She felt great. Hot, wet, ready for him.

He stroked his thumb across her clit as he slowly, ever so slowly, pumped in and out of her.

"Look at me, Araya. Do you like this? Is this what you want?"

Her beautiful, golden eyes swam with lust and emotion as she gazed up at him.

"Yes, "she whispered.

"You feel so good. I could stay inside you for eternity. Ask for anything you want and I'll give it to you."

"I need to know how it feels to...to come with you inside me," she finished, her cheeks pinkening but her gaze didn't leave his.

Her wish was his command. He increased the pressure and the pace of his strokes on her clit. She cried out as her breath hitched and her pussy muscles clenched around his cock. He knew she was close. He slammed deep inside her and held still letting her work his cock the way she wanted it, needed it.

"Yes, Kean," she wailed, her head thrashing back and forth. Every muscle in his body strained to the point of agony to keep from releasing his come. Her sexy body thrashing around so close to orgasm, drove him mad.

"You're so beautiful. So sexy. Tell me you love me, Araya."

Confusion clouded her eyes.

"It's your fantasy," he reminded her. He let go of one of her legs to lean in and kiss her. Deep. Passionate. Loving. He pulled back just a little. She gazed into his eyes.

"I love you," she whispered, then pulled him down for another kiss.

Kean was shocked by the emotions that raced through him when she said those words. He was more into the fantasy than he realized. "And I love you," he said. He'd never said that to anyone before. Anyone outside family anyway. It felt odd but right. Not as difficult as he'd always assumed it'd be.

He saw a tear slip from the corner of her eye and kissed it away. He gave her deep thrusts of his cock, filling her all the way. He felt the contractions on his cock become more frequent and her breathing became more rapid. Yeah, he wanted to feel her climax as he thrust deep inside her.

"That's it. Kean, please," she stammered.

"Come for me, Araya," he demanded.

"Yes, now. Harder," she wailed.

She gripped the sheets with one fist and dug her nails into his back with the other. Then she went utterly still, her eyes widening, her mouth opened and something akin to a scream came out. He'd have thought her in pain if he hadn't felt her orgasm drench his cock.

That was it, he could hold back no longer. He roared as he came hard, her cunt milking him, searing pleasure speared from his balls, through his shaft, out the tip of his cock.

He reached a hand between her and the bed and used the last of his energy to scoot them both fully onto the bed. He reluctantly withdrew from her, and they both moaned at the separation.

He kissed her forehead as he lay beside her draping an arm across her middle as they both fought to catch their breath.

"How do you feel?" he asked.

ARAYA'S BODY HUMMED with energy, partly from Kean's seed flowing through her body, partly from the ecstasy she'd experienced at his skilled hands. If she'd had a clue how magnificent sexual encounters could be, she'd never have held out for so many years.

"Exhilarated, content," she answered.

Maybe this *Sempire* thing wouldn't be so bad after all. No. Even though she felt her demon nature taking hold, she still wanted love, a forever relationship. She wanted it even more now that she'd had a taste of it with Kean. He'd fulfilled her fondest fantasy. She didn't know why but he'd known exactly what she wanted and he'd given it to her if only for a short time.

"Good," he said. "Me too. You are incredible."

She'd been so angry with him, she'd convinced herself she hated him but she knew now that was a lie. She couldn't hate the man who'd made her feel loved. Cherished. Adored. *He* was the incredible one.

Despite his betrayal, she truly enjoyed his company, liked him and desired him with a passion she'd never known she was capable of.

She'd let herself believe the illusions as he'd requested. She'd never known she had the ability to let her imagination take such a strong hold and make her feel, if only for a short time, that she had what she truly wanted. She wondered if she'd be able to continue fantasizing, to that degree, in the future so maybe she could fool herself into believing the lie but she knew in her heart she'd never meet another like Kean.

Her heart already mourned the loss, knowing she had to let him go, knowing she'd never experience that same depth of emotion again. Maybe she could see him again one day. No, it would be more difficult to let him go a second time but she would always carry with her the memory of what they'd shared tonight.

His breathing slowed and evened out, and she realized he'd fallen asleep, his arm still draped across her. She imagined falling asleep with him like this every night and her body hummed its approval. She stroked the light stubble on his cheek, careful not to wake him. She could easily get used to this intimacy and her heart ached knowing it was doubtful it'd ever happen again.

It was time to let him go.

She carefully slid from beneath his arm and off the bed. She picked up her robe from the floor, walked to the intercom and quietly requested her mother's presence.

Chapter Six

As the guard opened the door to Araya's room, she shoved past him and stood before her mother. She hadn't stepped outside her room for more than three months. It felt odd and exhilarating at the same time.

"What's the urgency dear? Is everything okay?" Talith looked her up and down. "I can feel your strength. You've fed again." She smiled and stepped forward then hesitated.

Araya needed to sell this if she wanted her mother to agree to Kean's release, so she threw her arms around her mother and hugged her tight. "Thank you. I feel better than I've ever felt."

Talith squeezed her tight then pulled back and stared. Araya kept the smile on her face. She knew her mother wasn't stupid and she could tell Talith was searching her face for signs of disingenuousness.

"Mother?" Araya said trying to keep her face from cracking from the plastered on smile.

Her mother relented and pulled her back into her arms for an enthusiastic hug. "Oh Araya. I am so happy for you. Happy for me." She pulled back and Araya was surprised to see tears in her mother's eyes. "I'm sorry for the... You do understand don't you? I couldn't bear to lose you. You are my daughter and I love you."

As pissed off as she was, she couldn't help but warm at those words. Her mother's methods had been ridiculous and dangerous but yes she did understand she'd been trying to save her child's life.

"I'm still a little upset by your methods." Araya admitted honestly. "I mean an Incubus, Mother? Really?"

Talith had the decency to look abashed. "It was a desperate move, yes."

"Well, the end result is this," she twirled around, "so no harm done. Plus, he was fantastic." Araya wondered if she was laying it on too thick.

"Come on," Talith grabbed her hand, "let's surprise your sister."

"Wait." Araya didn't know how long she could keep up this happy pretense. "Let's release Kean first."

Talith's gaze narrowed.

"No sense keeping him here longer than necessary. He's served his purpose. Besides, have you smelled him? I'm afraid if he sticks around much longer, I'll take him again and again. I'd really like to avoid addiction."

Talith nodded, seeming to buy her reason. "Good point, however, we'll need to make certain you're not already suffering addiction before releasing him."

Oh crap. "How can we tell?" she asked, trying to keep her voice from wavering.

"You'll need to feed from another. If addicted, you won't be able to. No one else will work for you."

Oh. Hell. No. *Think, Araya, think.* "I'm already drooling just thinking about the males Valia told me we'd scout out together. I don't think the mixed-breed is an issue for me. Yeah, he was great but I have nothing to compare him to. I'm sure there's better." Araya almost gagged on those words. She'd probably never have such a beautiful experience again and to demean it, even in jest, made her queasy.

Talith studied her for a moment and then agreed. "That train of thought tells me what I need to know. You'd be very reluctant to let him go if even slightly dependent on him. This is such a happy day for me. You will make a wonderful *Sempire*."

Araya forced herself to mirror her mother's jubilant gaze. "Thanks. Let's get him out of here and then find Valia and have a celebration."

KEAN HAD BEEN DISAPPOINTED to awaken to an empty bed, which wasn't the norm for him. He didn't typically stick around for a hell of a lot of cuddle time. A little, now and then, but not much. He told himself his disappointment was more because he figured the waking up together and cuddling would be part of Araya's fantasy. He only wanted to play it out to its fullest for *her* benefit. *Yeah, that was it.*

He'd thought maybe she'd slipped off to the bathroom when he heard a door close but that particular door was wide open. Then he'd heard the voices in the hallway. Another benefit of his demon DNA—better than human hearing. He strode to the door and concentrated on the voices.

He couldn't believe his fucking ears. "I don't think the mixed-breed is an issue for me. Yeah, he was great but I have nothing to compare him to. I'm sure there's better." Wow, talk about an ego crusher. And talk about a change in the once romantic female's attitude. Apparently, he'd done his job and done it well. Her *Sempire* nature must have already obliterated her human side.

What did it matter to him? Hell, he'd be released soon and could get back to his life. He should be ecstatic. So why did his gut feel like he'd been punched in it?

He jumped back a couple feet when the door handle turned. Araya stepped inside the room. He would swear her face lit up when she saw him standing there but that look was quickly replaced with a cool detachment.

"Kean," she said, no emotion laced her voice. "You can leave now."

Just like that, she dismissed him.

Talith stepped inside the room. "Darcon," she indicated the guard behind her with a wave of her hand, "will escort you outside the veil, remove the collar and then you're free."

Kean looked back and forth between Talith and Araya. Damn, he felt a little dirty and not in a good way. Used and dismissed. He needed to get the hell out of this place. He was turning into a girl.

He shot one last glance at Araya but she still showed no emotion. Fine. This was what he wanted, right? "Great," he said tersely, "it's about time. I'll need my clothes."

"Of course." Talith motioned to the guard and he disappeared. "Darcon will return in a moment with your clothes. Thank you for your *service* mixed-breed. Come Araya, let's find your sister."

Araya turned to leave with her mother. "Wait," Kean said.

She turned back to him and raised a questioning eyebrow. He had no idea what to say or why he'd stopped her.

"Nothing," he muttered.

Her expression softened a bit and she said, "Thank you." She hesitated and he thought he heard her voice hitch, "For *everything*." Then she quickly exited the room.

Kean still stood staring at the door when the guard entered the room a minute later. Darcon handed Kean his folded clothing, shoes and keys and he quickly dressed, eager to leave this place and these unwanted feelings behind.

"Follow me," the guard grumbled.

He followed the guard down the hallway then down the massive staircase almost running into Valia at the bottom.

"Hey, Incubus!" She greeted him with a laugh. "Where ya goin'?"

"Home," he answered tersely.

Valia's face turned into a picture of surprise. "Oh. I thought you'd be staying longer. Where's my sister?" she asked.

"Looking for you."

"Darcon, are you taking him through the veil?" He nodded in answer.

"I will take him," she volunteered then looped her arm through Kean's. Darcon stepped in front of them blocking their path but said nothing.

"Chill out. He's collared and I'm much stronger than him anyway," she told the guard.

That irked but he was man enough to admit it was probably true with her being full-blooded demon but his male ego whispered to him that he could take her if push came to shove.

Kean wondered what the hell she had planned. As gorgeous as she was, after the night he'd spent with her sister, he really wasn't up for *feeding* her. He needed to get back to women who wanted him solely for the pleasure he could provide them, not because they needed to *feed* off him.

When the guard didn't budge, Valia rolled her eyes. "Fine. Come with us but follow at a distance."

They walked through the grand foyer, the intricate fruit patterns etched into the polished concrete floors shone in the bright light streaming through the large windows on either side of the massive mahogany doors. The guard rushed ahead of them to open the door and held it open as they stepped outside into the veil. He'd never journeyed inside it before. The thick air enveloped him and seemed to push at him but like on Araya's balcony it wasn't unpleasant just different.

Valia let go of his arm and turned to face him. "I'm really surprised you're leaving so soon. Were you given the choice to stay?"

"Why so concerned about me leaving?" he asked.

She shrugged her shoulders. "Just curious."

"Bullshit."

She laughed. "I like you, Incubus. Have I mentioned that?"

He folded his arms across his chest. He didn't know what her game was and wondered if she knew something he didn't.

"I just got the feeling you'd want to stick around. That's all."

"Why the hell would I want to *stick around*? I didn't want to be here in the first place," he said.

"True," she agreed. "But I thought maybe Araya would convince you to stay."

"Araya couldn't wait to get me out of here," he ground out. That still burned even though he didn't care.

"What makes you think that?" she asked.

"I overheard her say so to your mother."

"Ah, I see," she said, pursing her lips. "Where is home, Incubus? I'll port you to the closest location possible. I assume you can't do it yourself."

Why did these females keep pointing out his undesirable characteristics?

"Anywhere near Texas," he answered. He didn't want to be too specific in case they ever decided to come after him for any reason. He had no idea why they would but he didn't need any demons knowing where he lived. Period.

She laughed at him. "Texas is a big state. You need to be a little more specific."

He opened his mouth to give her a destination at least one hundred miles from his home. He could take a cab once they parted ways. But she punched him, playfully, in the arm and spoke before he got the lie out.

"No need to be evasive. If I want to know where you live, you can lie all you want, I'll still find out." She laughed again. "And the more evasive you are, the more I want to know."

Fine. "Do you know Club Raze in Dallas? The one your mother abducted me from?" he asked.

"Actually, yes I do. I'll take you there," she said. She touched his hand and within seconds, they stood in the parking lot of the club. Darcon came forward and removed the collar from Kean's neck with, what seemed to be, only a brush of his fingers, then he distanced himself again.

Kean forced his body to steady. Teleporting wasn't his thing. He'd only ported a few times in his life with the assistance of some full-blooded demon associates of his father's. The porting didn't sit well with him then and it obviously still didn't because his stomach roiled and he had to fight the urge to puke. Luckily, his car was still here. It surprised him it hadn't been towed. Finally, something was going his way.

"HERE WE ARE," VALIA said. "So, uh, any parting words?"

"Bye," Kean answered as he walked to his car.

"Funny. Any message you'd like me to deliver to *anyone*?" She prompted.

He stopped and turned to face her. "What's up, *Sempire*? If you have something to say, say it. If not, I'm getting in my car and going home."

She put her hands on her hips. "Such a difficult Incubus," she sighed. "My father was a *Sensus* demon—an aura reader and manipulator. I retained the ability to read, a little anyway, after my transition."

"And?" Kean asked.

"I can read yours," she said, giving him a pointed look he didn't understand and then she disappeared.

He shook his head and got in his car, sitting there a moment, trying to figure out what Valia saw in his aura or whatever. When nothing registered but frustration, he jammed the keys in the ignition, put the car in gear and sped away toward home.

"THERE YOU ARE," ARAYA said, as Valia stepped into the dining room. Talith and Araya sat at the massive mahogany table piled high with platters of fruit.

"Where were you?" Talith asked. "We had to start the celebration without you."

"Flirting, groping. The usual." She shrugged and grabbed a chunk of pineapple and popped it into her mouth. "I heard the Incubus is gone."

Araya's chest tightened but she tried to keep her gaze level. She threw a handful of blueberries into her mouth as a distraction. "Yep. He's gone."

"How do you feel about that?" Valia asked.

Araya narrowed her eyes and shot her sister a look. She wondered if Valia was attempting to read her aura. "Fine."

"Good. You're ready to hit a club with me later tonight?" Valia asked.

What Araya really wanted to do was lock herself back in her room and pull the covers over her head. Or maybe drink a couple bottles of wine, then pull the covers over her head. She decided to keep up the pretense as long as she could though. "Maybe we can just hang out here tonight. Have a girl's night in. Fruit, wine, music, a movie?"

"What?" Valia asked, incredulous. "You've been stuck in your room for months. Let's go out. Drink. Dance. Flirt."

"Tomorrow, okay?" She used her best pleading look.

Valia's shoulders sagged in defeat. "Fine, party pooper."

"Araya," her mother's concerned voice cut in, "are you certain the Incubus isn't an issue?"

"Yes," Araya said quickly. "It's just... I've gone from half dead to this," she indicated herself with her hands, "overnight. I'm feeling pretty overwhelmed. I need a night to let it all sink in. An adjustment period."

Talith smiled at her and squeezed her hand. "Understandable. You'll be fine, dear."

"True. I didn't even consider that," Valia said. "Okay. Meet you in the theatre room in ten minutes. You pick the movie—anything with *eye candy*. I'm going to change my clothes."

Chapter Seven

"It's been four days, Araya. You're weakening. You have to come out with me tonight or... Fuck it. Or I'm going to tell Mother what's going on," Valia said, placing her hands on her hips defiantly.

"No! Valia, you can't tell her. I'll be fine." Araya tried to convince her sister.

"I haven't said anything yet because you're my sister and I love you. I know this whole thing is harder for you but I'm not going to watch you go downhill again. It'll be faster and more painful since you fed."

"I'm sure it'll pass in a day or two—," Valia cut her off.

"Tonight, Araya. You're going out with me tonight or I'll tell mother and she'll hunt the Incubus down, collar him and drag him back here. I'm tempted to do it myself."

"You wouldn't," Araya said, alarmed.

"Try me. Get dressed. I'll be back in thirty minutes." She stopped short of the door and turned, flashing a playful smile. "Wear something sexy."

She knew Valia meant what she said. Her sister didn't often get so pissy. She'd have to go with her tonight. No more excuses. Unless she wanted her mother to drag Kean back here. Which, of course, she didn't want that at all.

She dressed and applied a bare minimum of makeup. Her heart wasn't into to this. As promised, Valia returned in exactly thirty minutes.

Valia chose a club that skirted a thin spot in the veil in Texas. Valia told her clubs that closely skirted the thin spots were her favorites because they attracted demons as well as the more adventurous humans. Nice variety.

As they walked to the door, Araya's stomach knotted. She smoothed her hands down her dress. She considered making a run for it. But no, she could walk in the club, have a drink or five and wait for Valia to disappear with her male of the evening. Then, Araya would get the hell out of there.

"You look great, chick. Don't be nervous," Valia encouraged and grabbed her hand. "Look. I thought maybe you'd talk to me about it but you haven't. Maybe you're in denial. I don't know. But I know you care about—"

"Stop," Araya said. "I..." She opened her mouth to lie but instead said, "I need to forget about that, let it go."

Valia squeezed her hand and said, "Okay. Put a smile on your face. You never know what the night may bring."

The thumping music and pulsing lights assaulted her senses. Valia dragged her along behind her, weaving through the gyrating crowd, to the bar. She expertly maneuvered them into position to order drinks. As soon as the bartender caught sight of Valia, he ignored the patrons who'd been there ahead of them and made a beeline for her.

She ordered for both of them, and when the bartender delivered their drinks he slid Valia his phone number on a napkin. She leaned over the bar and whispered something in his ear that lit up his face as if he'd just won the lottery. Araya supposed he had won the sexual lottery if Valia picked him for the evening.

Valia handed her a drink and then she followed her to the back of the club where there were fewer people gyrating and more places to sit and relax. Valia hooked a chair with her stiletto-clad foot, pulled it out and sat. Araya followed suit.

"Whatcha think?" Valia asked.

Araya looked around then looked back to Valia. She had to speak loud to project her voice over the music.

"It's great," she answered lamely.

Valia rolled her eyes. "Chug your drink. I'll ask again when you have a buzz." She pointed to the dance floor. "If you see anything you like, don't be shy. I do and I'm going to dance. Be back in a minute."

Araya watched her sister strut over to a guy, human as far as she could tell, surrounded by three attractive women. Valia walked right up to him, took his hand and walked him to the dance floor as the women shot her daggers. The guy followed with no hesitation. She chuckled to herself. She'd kill to have that kind of confidence.

Araya downed her drink then polished off Valia's too. Screw it. She was in a club, sitting alone, she might as well catch a buzz. Besides, she needed a pick-me-up. She'd been feeling crappy all day, weakening again.

"What's a beautiful woman like you doing all alone?" A male voice asked from beside her, startling her.

She turned and looked up to see an attractive man smiling at her. Before she could speak, he pulled out a chair and sat down next to her. He extended his hand. "I'm Rick."

Araya had never done the flirting in a club thing with a random guy, but since Valia was staring at her from the dance floor, she figured she'd put on a show. She hoped her sister would think she'd chosen someone, be satisfied, take off with some dude and then Araya could go home. Alone.

She took his hand and said, "I'm Araya and I'm not alone. I'm here with my sister."

"Ah, where is she?" Rick asked.

Araya pointed toward the dance floor. "The extreme redhead."

Rick's eyes almost bugged out of his head when he caught sight of Valia. That irked even though Araya had no interest in this guy.

"Wow, two gorgeous sisters. Impressive. Wanna dance?"

Araya had only ever danced at home. Either alone in her room or at home with Valia. She'd slow danced with Fin a few times too, but this was not a slow dancing crowd and she hadn't danced with Valia the way these people were dancing. Half of them looked as though they were having sex with clothes on.

"I'm not much of a dancer," she said.

He stood and held his hand out to her. "It's easy. Come on."

She had no desire to dance with this guy. She had no desire to do anything with this guy. Shouldn't her *Sempire* side be making her crave him? Or someone else? She scented him and her body wanted him nutritionally but her mind rebuked the idea. She wasn't complaining but found it odd. It'd been four days since being with Kean.

Although she could scent Rick, while not totally appalling, he couldn't compare to Kean's mouth-watering scent.

Kean. She couldn't stop thinking about him. About the last night they'd spent together. He'd offered her her fantasy and she'd reveled in it. He'd made her feel loved. He'd made love to her. He'd made her want the fantasy more than she had before.

She shook her head as if it would stop the incessant thoughts of Kean and of what she'd never have. She needed a distraction and one stood in front of her. She accepted his outstretched hand and stood. Whoa. She wobbled when she stood. Those drinks must have been stronger than they'd tasted.. Yep, she was definitely tipsy. She'd only ever drank the wine that was specially created with fruit from their land.

Rick pulled her to him as they began to dance to the sensual beat of the music. He was handsome enough but she felt nothing. She closed her eyes and let herself go. They swayed and moved to the beat. Nothing.

She conjured an image of Kean and her body instantly warmed and she wrapped her arms around her dance partner. She imagined it was Kean's body molded to hers, his hands sliding down her back. Her body tingled and she ground her hips seductively.

"Yeah baby, that's it," a male voice said against her ear, startling her out of her fantasy.

She pulled back as she realized what she'd been doing. She wanted Kean and this guy was not him. She felt sick and sad and wanted to get the hell out of the club but Valia was still watching. She needed her sister to believe she was accepting her new life.

"What's wrong, baby?" Rick said.

I'm not your baby, asshole. "I'm thirsty. I'm going to get another drink."

He grabbed her arm and said, "What're you drinking? I'll get it."

She shrugged out of his grip and said, "Anything fruity."

He nodded. "Back in a minute."

Araya went back to the table and sat. Valia was suddenly there. She plopped down on the seat next to Araya. "So," she asked curiously, "how's it going? Who's the dude? Is he the one?"

The one. I wish. She forced a smile on her face for Valia's benefit. "He'll do."

Valia's perfect pink lips formed a pout. "He'll do? That's not very exciting. Especially for your first time. Well, your first time out of the house and on your own. Someone better will come along."

Araya doubled over, clutching her stomach. As quickly as the pain had started, it stopped.

"Oh shit," Valia said. "You waited too long." She looked around the club as if searching for something, then looked back to Araya. "I should have insisted you come last night."

"What the hell was that?" Araya asked, concerned.

"Stabbing pain in the stomach? And you've been dizzy?"

Araya nodded. "A little unsteady here and there."

"You need a male. It's going to get worse. The gradual decline you experienced before was nothing compared to what you'll experience now. Araya, by tomorrow, you'll be in terrible pain and be as weak as you were before the Incubus." Valia's voice hitched.

The Incubus. Araya wondered what Kean was doing right now? Had he thought of her since he'd left? Was he in a club, such as this one, sweeping some woman off her feet? Was he already inside her, pleasuring her with his body?

Araya felt another stab in the gut, but it wasn't pain from lack of semen. She wished she didn't care what he was doing or who. He'd simply been a male her mother had forced to be with her. He'd played his part wonderfully in her fantasy, but that was all it had been. A fantasy. It was over and she needed to get used to it.

She just wanted to get the hell out of here, away from people, away from everyone. Rick chose that minute to show up with her drink. She leaned over and whispered in Valia's ear. "Go ahead and take care of your business. I'll make do with this guy for tonight," she lied.

Valia looked around the club again. Searching.

"Um. No. Don't jump into it with this guy. He obviously isn't doing it for you." Valia bit her lip as her eyes darted around the club some more.

Wait. What? Valia wanted her to do this, had been badgering her to do this. Had threatened her with her mother if she didn't come out and now she was poo-pooing Araya's *choice* of male?

Rick handed Araya her drink while quite obviously eyeballing Valia. *Asshole.* He tried to introduce himself to Valia but she stood and blew him off. Just like that. She bent and told Araya to chill for a few minutes and she'd be back.

He pulled his chair right next to Araya's, leaned in and put his hand on her knee. Yuck. She downed her drink in one gulp.

"Whoa baby, I like the way you drink."

She leaned forward, their faces, only inches apart. "My name is *Araya*."

Oh god. Her mouth began watering and her stomach clenched. That smell. So familiar. So irresistible. She must be too far gone, her demon nature making her think this guy was giving off Kean's scent, making sure she couldn't resist, couldn't starve herself any longer.

"Yeah but you're my baby tonight."

Yuck.

Before she knew what he was going to do, he reached behind her head and pulled her to him and planted a kiss on her lips. Her stomach churned and she pulled back from him. He didn't seem to notice her repulsion. "Wanna get out of here?"

Before she could tell the guy to get lost, that tangy scent assaulted her, making her salivate. It definitely wasn't coming from this guy.

"I SEE YOU'VE ACCEPTED your new life."

Araya whipped her head around at the sound of the most seductive voice she'd ever heard. Her bones melted as her eyes focused on him. "Kean. What are you doing here?"

"Apparently interrupting," he said and turned to leave.

Araya jumped to stop him but she swayed on her feet. "Wait." The room spun and her vision went fuzzy. She shouldn't have gulped that last drink. She tried to take another stepped forward but her legs weren't cooperating and she stumbled. Kean turned just in time to catch her. His hands ignited a fire inside her.

God she wanted him. There was no denying it. Her body demanded she throw her arms around him. Kiss him. Take him into her mouth. But she couldn't function properly. She'd never felt this way from drinking before. It must be a combination of weakening and the alcohol.

He lowered her back onto the chair and she held onto the table for support. "I don't know what's wrong with me," she slurred.

Kean looked at Araya then to the table and back at the guy. "Not drinking tonight?" he asked.

Rick stood. He was tall, but not as tall and not as muscled as Kean. "What's it to you?" he asked.

Kean reached over and picked up Araya's empty drink. He sniffed it then swiped his finger inside the glass and sucked his finger.

Even through blurred eyes, Araya saw Kean go rigid and a black mask drape his expression. He grabbed Rick around the neck with his free hand.

"You drugged her?" he asked, a menacing tone in his voice.

Rick's eyes bugged as he unsuccessfully struggled to loosen Kean's hold on his neck.

"Get the fuck out of here before I kill you." Kean's voice was nothing but a growl. "If I ever see you again, I *will* kill you." He shoved Rick hard enough that he stumbled backward and fell on his ass. He scrambled to get up and made a beeline for the door.

"He drugged me?" Araya squeaked.

Valia and Fin showed up at that moment. "Fin? What're you doing here?" Araya asked, confused.

"Doing your sister a favor. Are you okay?"

"She's been drugged," Kean announced. To her he said, "Next time you might want to let your *meal* know up front that you're a sure thing." Then he stormed away.

The scorn in his voice cut straight through her bones. She disgusted him. What she was disgusted him. Had she not been so woozy she'd have run after him and let him know she hadn't been with anyone since him. That she didn't want anyone but him. Pointless? Maybe. But she didn't want this to be their last interaction.

"Come on. Let's get you some air, walk it off." Fin said as he and Valia helped her up and supported her.

"I can't believe that asshole drugged you," Valia said angrily. Then her expression brightened, and she asked, "Are you high? Maybe I should find him and steal his stash."

Nice. So much for her first night out on the town.

KEAN NEEDED A FIGHT or a fuck. Seeing Araya kiss that guy made his blood boil. He'd wanted to snap the dude's neck before he knew he'd drugged her. Fucking prick. He should have killed him. Should have ripped his balls off and shoved them down his throat.

He'd been both reluctant and excited to come here tonight. Fin had shown up at Kean's door, surprising the hell out of him and had insisted Kean go out with him tonight. Of course, he'd refused Fin's invitation. Just because the male had made him a steak dinner didn't mean Kean wanted to party with him.

Obviously, Valia or the guard had followed him home the other day. Sneaky demons.

When Kean refused to show up at the club Fin insisted he visit, Fin spilled. He'd said Araya needed to see him and that it was urgent. He'd asked Fin what was so urgent but Fin swore he didn't know, only that she was *desperate* to see him.

Yeah, his dick and his ego kept kicking him in the ass lately. Hearing that she *needed* him and was *desperate* to see him was all it took for his chest to puff up—his cock too—and then he agreed to go to the club.

He'd spotted her within minutes of arriving. She sat there looking stunning in that form-fitting dress and he'd had to fight the desire to keep from running to her. Then that prick sat down next to her. Kean had thought maybe it was some random dude sitting down to hit on her until she'd leaned toward him and they kissed.

His gut twisted into knots at seeing that. He'd almost turned and walked away then but was glad he didn't after realizing what that son-of-a-bitch had tried to do to Araya.

Had Finn been toying with him by telling him Araya wanted to see him? Why would he do that? He'd told Araya he'd been doing her sister a favor and the redhead was a strange one. Was she playing games for her amusement at his expense?

He seriously needed to relieve some stress. His entire body was tense and there was a rage inside him. He should have at least beaten that dude within an inch of his life.

His thoughts were cut off by the sight of Fin and Valia helping Araya out of the club. Even though he knew those two could and would take care of her, he felt like an ass for not offering assistance. He'd been so consumed with rage, he'd just walked away.

Shit. He wanted her. Anger and need pulsed through him. He'd missed her. He wanted to be inside her again. Once wasn't enough. He strode to where they stood.

"Real nice, Incubus. Just walk away from a girl in distress. I don't think I like you anymore," Valia said, pouting.

"Kean?" Araya breathed.

Kean directed his response at Valia. "I need to speak with her. Alone." As he attempted to take Araya's arm, Fin stuck his huge arm between him and Araya.

"I don't think so. You blew it."

Araya put an unsteady hand on Fin's arm. "It's okay," she slurred.

Fin gave Kean a look, then reluctantly backed off as Kean swept her up into his arms. "I'm taking her to my car so she can sit down and listen," he threw the words over his shoulder as he carried her away.

He put her feet on the ground but kept a protective arm around her as he unlocked and opened the door and then helped her slide onto the seat and lie back. He buckled her seat belt to help keep her upright. When she was situated, he closed her door and walked around to the driver's seat and settled in. He didn't have a plan. Didn't know what he would say.

Before realizing what he was doing, he twisted the keys in the ignition and sped the hell away from the club, away from Fin and Valia.

"Kean, where're we going?"

"I don't know," he growled. "What the hell were you doing with that guy?" Okay. Stupid question. He knew exactly what she was doing with that guy. What did he expect? Her to mourn the loss of the part-Incubus who helped turn her into what she didn't want to be? Stupid.

From his peripheral vision, he saw her head sway as he took a corner a little too fast. She righted herself with some effort.

"I didn't know he'd drug me. Am I gonna be okay?"

"You should be more careful. Human drugs shouldn't have much effect on a demon but considering you're half human..." He paused, thinking about that. "Are you still half-human or does the *Sempire* gene obliterate the human DNA once you've *fed*?"

She shrugged. "Dunno. Mother and Valia were always sure I'd change after... But I don't feel different. Stronger, more alive, but not different in *that* way."

"What do you mean?" He noticed her words were already slightly less slurred.

"I mean I don't think any differently than I did before about what kind of life I want," she said quietly.

He glanced over at her, her golden eyes meeting his more steadily. Her demon DNA must already be negating the effects of the drug. Good.

"That must make it hard for you." Shit. After overhearing her talking to her mother in the hallway, he'd thought for sure she'd changed. Had it just been a show to satisfy her mother? Had she been trying to get him released because she felt bad for him? No. More likely she had wanted to get him out of her life because he'd gotten her to cave in to her desires.

And now he felt like a bigger ass knowing her thinking on the matter hadn't changed. She still wanted what she couldn't have.

Kean turned the car to the left. He'd take her to his home. What was he thinking anyway, taking off with her like that? Valia and Fin obviously knew where he lived and would come for her soon.

Kean's phone vibrated in the console. He picked it up and answered even though he didn't recognize the number. "Yeah?"

"Incubus, whatcha doin' with my sister?" Valia's voice sing-songed the question.

"How'd you get my number?" he asked in surprise.

"Duh. I'm awesome and resourceful. Now how about you answer my question."

"Talking."

"Hmmm. Was hoping for a sexier answer but whatever. Just know that I'll make you wear your insides on your outside if anything bad happens to her. Have fun."

She clicked off before he had a chance to respond and he had no doubt she meant what she said. She must believe he had no ill intentions toward her sister or she'd have been upset. She certainly wouldn't tell him to have fun.

As he pulled the car into the driveway, he said, "Your sister is strange."

"Yes, she is," Araya agreed. "That was her?"

"Yes."

"How'd she get your number?"

"Apparently she is *awesome and resourceful.*"

"That sounds like her," Araya giggled then asked, "Where are we?"

"My home."

He got out of the car, walked around, opened the door for her and extended his hand.

Instead of taking his hand, she asked, "Why am I here, Kean?"

"So we can talk," he said lamely. Hell, he'd been so worked up he hadn't thought this through. He only knew he wanted to be alone with her. Wanted to protect her.

"About what?"

"Come on," he said. He ducked down and unfastened her seat belt and hooked his hands under her arms lifting her from the seat, swinging her up into his arms again, he carried her to the front door.

"I'm feeling steadier now. You don't need to carry me. Guess you were right about the demon DNA." A loud hiccup punctuated her sentence and her cheeks turned pink. "I might still be a little tipsy though."

Damn her for being adorable. He set her down but held onto her arm as they walked inside.

Chapter Eight

Araya could not believe she was walking through Kean's door. She'd never expected to see him again. Out of all the clubs, in all the world, Valia had picked one less than fifteen minutes from Kean's house? No way was that a coincidence. Now that the fog had lifted from her brain, she realized Valia had set her up apparently with Fin's help. She was going to kill them both when she got home. Or maybe kiss them. She hadn't decided yet.

Kean lead her through the arched entry way into a masculine living room—all black leather furniture and beige walls—and indicated for her to take a seat on the couch. He needed some color in his life. If she lived here, she'd add plants and maybe some bright pillows on the couch and chairs. She mentally slapped herself. It'd do her no good to think that way.

"I'll be right back," he said as he made his way to the kitchen.

Araya devoured Kean with her eyes. His firm ass flexed beneath his jeans with each long stride. And God he smelled good. Being here was not a good idea. Images of her ripping his pants off and sucking him battled with images of her ripping his pants off and straddling him. Sinking down on his hard cock and milking him.

She hungered for him in so many ways. The *Sempire* need being one of them, yes. But she wanted more. She wanted the fantasy with him.

When he came back, he placed a platter full of blueberries and mango slices on the shiny black coffee table in front of her. "Hungry?" he asked. "Eat some. Clear your head."

She reached out and grabbed a slice of mango and stuffed it in her mouth. "Yum. You always have mango and blueberries on hand?"

He shifted awkwardly then took a seat next to her on the couch. "I started buying them after leaving your place."

She was drowning in his tangy male scent. She shoved a couple more mango slices in her mouth to keep herself from eating *him*. Her head swam from need. Oh shit. She clutched her stomach as another stabbing pain shot through her.

"Araya? What's wrong?"

"Kean," she started her voice throaty, "I should go."

She sat up and both loved and hated the concern she saw in his eyes.

"Tell me what's wrong," he demanded.

"I need... I need to go." She stood and swayed.

Kean jumped to his feet and wrapped his arms around her. He felt good. So warm and strong. She gazed up into his dark eyes.

"Your pupils are dilated." He lowered his face closer to hers. "And your scent..." He growled low in his throat. "You need sex."

She closed her eyes and her chin dropped. She felt ashamed and tried to pull from his grasp. But he held her tighter.

"Look at me," he said, his voice gravelly and she obliged with reluctance. "I know what you are. You don't have to be embarrassed. I... Do you...." A frown set on his lips and his muscles went rigid. His voice sounded strained as he gritted out, "Do you need me to take you back to the club to find a male?"

"What? No!" She couldn't believe he'd asked her that and she pushed out of his grip. He didn't offer himself, but offered to find her someone else? Damn, she knew he'd been forced into the situation with her in the beginning but he'd seemed to enjoy being with her. "Why did you bring me here if you find me so repulsive?"

He blanched as if she'd slapped him. "Repulsive? What I find repulsive is the idea of you with another male," he ground out. "But you..." he put his hands on either side of her face and looked into her eyes for a long moment, then kissed her with force. Their lips crashed together and his tongue plunged inside her mouth. He tasted so good. She'd longed to feel his kiss again.

He broke the kiss, his breathing ragged. "I find irresistible. I haven't been able to think straight since leaving you."

She sucked in a surprised breath. Could she have heard him correctly? "Really?" The word came out a squeak.

"Araya, let me take care of you tonight. Let me meet your needs." His jaw clenched as he gritted his teeth. "I know you've settled in to your *Sempire* life and want to continue experiencing other males." His hands tightened on her face almost to the point of pain. "But use me tonight. Let me touch you. Let me inside you. Let me feed you."

Araya could not believe her ears. Kean wanted her. Not because he was abducted and collared and it was his only hope for escape. He just wanted her. Did he care for her? No. She couldn't let her mind travel down that path. For now, it was enough that he wanted her with no ulterior motives.

And god, how she wanted him. She pulled his head down to her and kissed him with everything she had. His words fueled her desire. Every sweep of his tongue shot white-hot flame through her body.

"I'm taking that as acceptance of my offer," he said as he scooped her into his arms and carried her to his bedroom. He set her on the bed, kneeled down and removed her shoes. His hands slowly smoothed up her legs, leaving a warm tingling sensation in their wake.

"Wait," she struggled to get the word out. Kean stopped touching her immediately and a sigh escaped her lips. She took his hands in hers and encouraged him to sit beside her. "I don't want to *use* you, Kean."

He visibly tensed but she quickly explained. "I mean, I want you."

"Of course you do," he said tersely. You're a *Sempire*. I'm a male and part Incubus."

"No. I mean, yes. But what I'm trying to say is that I missed you." She turned away embarrassed by her admission but she wanted him to know. She wanted him to know that she didn't only want him to feed from him. She wanted *him*. The person. The man. The lover.

He audibly exhaled and pulled her to him so that she straddled him, her legs wrapped around his waist. She felt his erection pressing against her pussy, his jeans and her skimpy panties an annoying barrier. He brushed a light kiss across her lips, then stood and let her slide down his body until she stood in front of him. He grabbed the hem of her dress and pulled it up and over her head, then tossed it to the floor. He sucked in a breath as he looked at her, his eyes dark with desire.

"Irresistible." He dipped his head and sucked her nipple into his mouth.

She arched into him needing more contact. She needed this. Needed him.

He replaced his mouth with his hand, taking her other nipple into his mouth licking and teasing it to a taut peak. He eased her onto the bed and removed her panties then shed his own clothes, his muscles rippling as he removed his jeans.

She ached for him, burned for his touch. The sight of his thick. veined erection had her growling and she wanted him inside her. Inside her mouth. Inside her body. She cried out as another pain shot through her.

Kean moved to her side in an instant. "What is it?"

Araya covered her face with her hands. She wanted to savor this moment with him but she was losing it and she needed to feed *now*. She could barely keep herself from throwing him down and sucking the life out of him.

Another pain struck. She needed him now. She pushed him down on his back. "I'm sorry," she said.

HER USUALLY SOFT, SWEET voice was barely recognizable as she pushed him down, her strength surprising him. He wasn't sure he could fight her off even if he wanted to, which he did fucking *not* want to. Her pupils were so dilated the gold was barely visible. Her scent washed over him in heavy waves making him drunk with desire. Her need was so strong. He wondered if this insane need was a daily thing. He instantly shoved those thoughts from his mind. He didn't want to think about her wanting this so desperately with anyone but him.

She straddled him and began fumbling to get his cock inside her.

"Hey," he said, "slow down, no rush."

She growled at him. An actual animal-like growl. And it was fucking hot. She grabbed his cock—hard—guiding it to her slick cunt.

She slammed her body down, taking every inch of him inside her in a split second. He groaned as her moisture coated him, her channel enveloping him. She cried out and he thought she hurt herself, but then she rocked back and forth, bucking wildly on his dick. Her nails dug into his ribs as she fucked him.

Since leaving her, he'd been discontent, sullen and lonely. He'd tried to distract himself, but the usual parties and women didn't appeal to him. He'd missed the feel of her, the smell of her, her smile. *Her*. Being inside Araya felt like home. There was no place he'd rather be.

He'd never had a female ride him with such wild abandon. Her head thrashed from side to side, her golden hair whipping around her. *So fucking beautiful.* She alternated between thrusting her hips back and forth and bouncing up and down. The thought she might break his dick crossed his mind, but he was so lost in the pleasure of watching her and feeling what only she could do to him, he didn't care.

He watched his shaft slide in and out of her, shiny from her juices. Her perky breasts bouncing in time with her frenzied rhythm.

Oh fuck. He felt the semen fighting to burst from his wonderfully abused dick. He didn't want to come so fast. Didn't want it to be over.

As if she knew how close he was, she demanded in that animalistic tone, "Release it. Now." Her eyes showed no gold now. They'd turned completely black.

He did as ordered because he couldn't hold back against the assault her hot, tight cunt waged on his shaft. Every muscle in his body tensed as he exploded, roaring as jet after hot jet of his release spurted into her.

He felt her walls clench around him and she fell forward onto him as she cried out. "Oh Kean. Oh god." He rocked inside her as she climaxed, her slick walls spasming, milking him.

They lay there trying to catch their breath. Her body still slumped over him and her face tucked into his neck. He smoothed her sweat dampened hair away from her face and placed a light kiss on her forehead.

"I'm sorry," she said.

"Sorry? For what?"

"For... For just taking you. Oh my god. What did I do?"

He chuckled. He couldn't help himself. She sounded so serious. "Araya, I have never experienced anything quite like that, and I can tell you I enjoyed every second of it."

She lifted her head and looked in his eyes. "Really?"

He took her face in his hands and said, "Yes. Really. I've never seen anything so sexy. You needed me and you took me."

She frowned and buried her face in his shoulder again. "But I didn't want to use you."

"Is that all it was about? Did you not want me before the need took over?"

"I've wanted you every day since you left," she admitted.

He wrapped his arms around her and squeezed her into him. He'd swear his heart stopped beating when she'd said that. He didn't want this to be over, didn't want her to leave.

"Araya, stay with me tonight. Let me make love to you now."

TONIGHT. She wanted nothing more than to stay with him but wished for more than tonight. She couldn't imagine ever finding another male who made her feel so much. Pleasure, happiness, completeness with him. Loneliness, longing, pain without him. But she'd take tonight and treasure it.

He rolled her over and kissed her deeply, licking and caressing every inch of her body, making her burn and feel treasured. He then made love to her slow and easy bringing them both to climax again, filling her with his seed, nourishing her inside and out.

She sighed as he pulled out of her. The loss of him in her depths made her feel empty. He turned on his side and pulled her into him so that her back and butt were cradled against him and his arms wrapped around her.

She wanted him to know, needed him to know. "You're still the only male who's touched me," she whispered.

He moved away from her just enough to turn her over and look into her eyes. "How is that possible?"

She felt a tear slide down her cheek. "I couldn't."

"Goddamn it, Araya. You're actually addicted to my—to me? You should have come to me. I would have helped you through it."

She put her fingers on his lips to shut him up. "I couldn't because I wanted *you*. The last night we spent together—I knew I'd never feel that with anyone else."

His face softened and he wiped the stray tear from her cheek. "Your *Sempire* nature didn't wipe out your human desires. You still want the fantasy."

Yes, he was right but there was more. She couldn't bring herself to say it. She wasn't addicted to him because of his Incubus semen. She'd never felt so close to anyone as she did to him tonight. Not even the night they'd played out her fantasy together. Tonight, the feelings between them had been real. He'd made love to her with no ulterior motives. It was just him and her. And, she couldn't bear rejection right now.

"Yes."

He hugged her to him and kissed the back of her head. She loved the feel of his heartbeat on her back.

After several long minutes, Kean spoke. "I'm sorry you suffered but I'm glad you didn't go to another male." His voice hardened. "I know you found one tonight but..."

She turned her head to him. "No. I didn't want him."

He scowled. "Maybe not but you were going to use him anyway. I saw you kissing him."

She turned over so she was facing him fully. He sounded so angry. Could it be? He said he found it repulsive to think of her with other males.

"Were you jealous?" she asked and held her breath in anticipation of his answer. If he said no, she'd die from embarrassment, but if he said yes, didn't that mean he cared? At least a little?

"Hell yes," he admitted. I've never been jealous a day in my life until meeting you. When I saw you kissing him, I wanted to rip his face off."

Araya was shocked by his admission and also elated.

"I didn't kiss him. He kissed me and it made me sick."

His brow furrowed. "Araya, are you sure you're not suffering addiction? How often do *Sempires* need to feed?"

"Every two or three days," she sighed.

"If you weren't with anyone after me that means it's been four days for you. Wouldn't your demon have driven you to feed?"

"You know I don't want that." She lowered her eyes. "Except with you."

"As much as it makes me happy to hear that, it doesn't make sense. I'm not an expert on your species but I thought once initiated, the need would drive you to do what you need to do. Unless you're addicted to an Incubus."

Damn him. Why couldn't he let it go?

"Araya?" he urged when she didn't answer right away.

"I might have been *driven*. I don't know." She shuddered.

"So you're sure you're not addicted? Especially after tonight?"

"Kean, honestly, I don't know but the reason I didn't want anyone else, is because..." She couldn't believe the next words that came out of her mouth. "I'm in love with you," she finished.

His sharp intake of breath made her envious because currently she couldn't breathe. Her lungs froze as she'd said those words. Her heart might have stopped beating too.

He gawked at her for what seemed like an eternity, then finally smiled and kissed her. A soul scorching, mind scrambling kiss.

When he pulled back, he rested his forehead against hers. "Stay with me, Araya. I know the risk to you is great, but we'll be in the same boat because I believe I'm addicted to you. To your touch, to your scent, to your smile, to your strength, to your mind. I haven't been able to think about another woman since being with you. For an Incubus, even only an eighth Incubus, that's impressive."

Finally, she breathed. He felt more for her than she thought possible. It wasn't a confession of love, and that saddened her, but it was probably for the best as the situation hadn't changed. She was what she was and the day would come that he'd be away for too long and she'd turn to another.

But wait, if she did become addicted to him she wouldn't be able to. Of course, then she'd suffer horrible pain and eventually die. Neither of the scenarios was ideal.

I'M IN LOVE WITH YOU. Emotion welled up inside him when she'd said those words. He'd heard it from other women when they were in the heat of passion, but he'd never heard it from someone who meant it, and he knew she did. He could feel it in her touch and see it in her eyes.

This beautiful, sweet, sexy *Sempire* loved him and he wasn't letting her go. *Ever*.

He could see the conflict in her eyes now and wanted to put her at ease.

"Araya, I know your concerns but I have no intention of ever being away from you long enough to make you suffer. It would make me suffer too." He brushed a light kiss on her lips.

"But what if it's unavoidable?" she asked, fear shining in her golden eyes.

"I'm not letting you go because of a what if."

"But you might tire of me after a while. It's not as if you're in love with me," her voice cracked and she looked away from him.

"What?" He grasped her chin and turned her face toward him. "I told you I loved you four days ago."

"Yes, but you were only pretending."

"I thought I was. I thought I was playing out the love fantasy for you, because I felt guilty and wanted to give you something special to remember. But as soon as the words came out of my mouth, I knew I wasn't pretending. It felt so right. Yeah, I'd been trying to lie to myself, trying to convince myself it was all for your benefit. But *that* was the lie. Araya, I'm seventy-three years old and I have *never* said those words to another woman. Never thought I would. So when I say it to you, please believe me."

Her eyes widened and her mouth dropped open.

"Oh my god. You're seventy-three? You're way too old for me," she said, sounding horrified.

That was *not* the reaction he expected. Shit. For a demon, seventy-three was nothing. He'd never thought twice about his age until this moment. He didn't look older than thirty and wouldn't for many years to come.

Araya chose that moment to burst out laughing. "You should see the look on your face," she choked out through the laughter.

She was teasing him. *Little shit.* He hadn't paid much attention to her ass during their love making but he'd remedy that right now. He sat up and pulled her across his lap, face down.

"What are you doing?" She squealed, still laughing at him.

"This old demon is going to give this young demon a spanking for laughing at her elder, that's what," he said as he popped her on her deliciously round ass cheek.

"Ow!" She wailed.

"That's what you get for joking during my confession of love."

He turned her over and pulled her up so that she sat across his lap and his lips met hers in an urgent kiss.

"Stay with me, Araya. Let me love you. Always."

"Always," she murmured against his lips.

ARAYA AWOKE CURLED into Kean's warm body, his arms wrapped around her. For the first time in her life, she looked forward to her future. A future with someone she loved, who loved her in return. She didn't fool herself into thinking everything would be perfect, that there wouldn't be obstacles along the way, but together they would make it work.

She stroked his arm and he kissed the back of her head. She rolled over to face him and he treated her to a sleepy, sensual smile.

"Morning," he said as he brushed a stray lock of hair from her face.

"Morning," she returned. "I was afraid to wake up and find out last night was a dream."

"It was," he said. "A dream we'll be living together. Let's dream some more right now," his lips lifted in a wicked grin as his hand caressed seductively down her body.

Kean growled as the doorbell rang.

"Expecting someone?" Araya asked, disappointment lacing her voice.

"No, ignore it," he said as his fingers slid between her legs making her shiver.

They both jerked upright as banging rang through the room, sounding as if someone was attempting to break down the front door.

"What the fuck?" Kean said. He scrambled from the bed and stormed to a large black dresser and pulled out a pair of black gym shorts pulling them on quickly.

Araya followed him out of bed, worried at the banging going on. It sounded serious. Kean sucked in a breath as his gaze fell on her nakedness.

"I'm going to kill the person responsible for making me wait to touch you," he growled. He fumbled through another drawer and pulled out a deep green t-shirt and tossed it to her.

She pulled it over her head. It bagged on her and fell to just above her knees, but she liked the idea of wearing something of his. It was somehow intimate.

The banging continued as she followed him through the foyer to the front door. He peered through the peephole and groaned.

"Unbelievable," he ground out as he unlocked and yanked the door open.

"Morning, Incubus! We were about to break down your door," Valia announced happily.

She pushed past him, Fin right behind her carrying two large bags over his shoulders and what the hell? A deformed dog bounded in behind them. Crooked eyes, lopsided ears and misshapen body.

"Nice shirt." Valia said winking at Araya. "So give me the tour."

Before Kean could ask what was wrong with the poor dog, it transformed into Kiberry. "It's a shifter?" he asked no one in particular.

Araya answered as she leaned forward to rub the beast's furry head. "He," she corrected him again. "And yeah, he's still learning. He hasn't quite gotten the hang of it yet."

"No shit," Kean said.

"Valia, Fin, what are you doing here?" Araya asked bewildered.

"I'm checking on my little sister. You look good, happy. So, I guess his," she pointed at Kean, "insides are safe."

"Insides?" Araya asked.

"Never mind." she grinned at Kean. "Hey Fin, looks like we can use bag number two." She walked past them as if she owned the place. "Where's a table? Ah, here we go," she said as she found the dining area. Araya hadn't noticed the shiny black table and six matching chairs last night. She realized *she* needed a tour of Kean's—*their*—home.

Their home. The thought warmed her.

Fin joined Valia at the table and set one bag on the floor and emptied the contents of the other on the table. A scrumptious looking platter of blueberries and mango—Araya's favorites—and pineapple and kiwi—Valia's favorites—made her stomach growl. Next came four plastic cups with lids, containing what she knew to be Fin's specialty fruit smoothies made with nothing more than ice and the freshest fruit from their gardens. Araya would miss that, but supposed she could visit and gather fruit any time.

"This is for us," he told Kean and lifted the lid on the last platter. It contained steak, eggs, biscuits and blueberry pancakes.

"What is all this?" Kean asked, a bewildered look on his face.

"Geez, Incubus," Valia rolled her eyes at him, "it's called breakfast. Everyone sit down. Let's eat."

Kean arched an eyebrow at Araya and she shrugged then stood on her tiptoes to brush a light kiss on his lips before sitting down.

"This looks fantastic," Kean said, "but you could have called first. I had other plans for breakfast."

Araya felt her face flame.

Valia laughed and said, "I bet you did."

"So what's in the other bag?" Araya asked.

"Various sharp instruments," Fin answered cryptically.

She didn't miss the grin Fin and Valia shared.

Everyone piled their plates high with food and Kiberry made a huffing, grumbling sound and pawed at Kean's leg.

"Uh, what does it—*he* want?" Kean asked.

"Incubus, I'm beginning to wonder about your intelligence level. He wants food," Valia informed him in her ever so *not* charming way.

Kean pulled off a piece of blueberry pancake and tossed it. The beast snatched it out of the air and swallowed it whole. He'd think with teeth like those, the beast might bother to chew a little.

Valia said, "Tell us about last night. How'd it go? I see Araya looks good and," she snickered, "nourished."

Araya choked on her mango slice. "Valia!"

"What? You do." Her eyes widened innocently.

Araya wasn't sure how Valia or her mother would take the news of her having a monogamous relationship, living with one man, part Incubus nonetheless. She didn't have the words to express it at the moment and was grateful Kean apparently did.

Kean swallowed a forkful of eggs then announced to Valia and Fin, "Araya and I will be getting married. That's how it went. Does that work for you?" He didn't give her time to answer. "Good. Because I love her and she loves me, and I won't allow anyone or anything to stand in the way of that."

Valia's mouth dropped open. Fin's mouth dropped open. Kiberry pawed at Kean's leg. Araya's heart seized.

"Married?" Araya squeaked.

"Of course." Kean took her hands in his. "I thought you understood that when I asked you to stay with me always. You will marry me won't you?"

Araya felt the tears of happiness streaming downing her cheeks. She couldn't believe this was happening. "Yes, I will."

Valia finally found her voice. "Holy shit. You'll probably be the first *Sempire* in the history of time to get *married.* Wow! Mom's going to freak."

"Congratulations," Fin offered looking genuinely happy for them. "I'd be happy to cater the wedding."

"I'd like to send your mother a fruit basket to thank her for abducting me," Kean said, smiling at Araya.

Laughter broke out around the table.

"Hey, if I'm going to be visiting my sister here, you're going to have to let her add some color to this place. It's nice, but all this black is depressing. And how much land do you have here? You need some fruit trees," Valia announced.

"We have fifty acres at our disposal. We'll contact a landscaper today." He turned to Araya and took her hands in his. "You request anything you want and we'll have them get started on a fruit garden right away. This is your home now as much as mine."

Araya's heart filled with more happiness than she'd ever known. *Her home. Their home.* Life was good and would only get better.

The End

From the author

THANKS SO MUCH FOR reading!

If you enjoyed the story, I'd love it if you left a quick review. Also, you can continue the Sempire Seductions Series with Valia's Villain and Fin's Fantasy!

About the Author

Jocelyn writes paranormal and contemporary romances that include humor, lust, love, and four-letter words on the way to a Happily-Ever-After.

Visit Jocelyn online @ JocelynDex.com

Don't miss out!

Visit the website below and you can sign up to receive emails whenever Jocelyn Dex publishes a new book. There's no charge and no obligation.

https://books2read.com/r/B-A-JUDF-NIHQ

BOOKS 2 READ

Connecting independent readers to independent writers.

Also by Jocelyn Dex

Sempire Seductions
Araya's Addiction
Valia's Villain
Fin's Fantasy

Sexy Zombie Tales
A Zombie Ate My Panties
My Zombie Valentine
Trick or Zombie
Sexy Zombie Tales: Books 1-3

Standalone
Gettin' Lucky with a Leprechaun
Assistant Seduction
Sempire Seductions
A Demon's Gift
Riding Dasher
Nasty Neighbor
Lying for Love
Belize Nights
Urban Coyote